The Bachelor Bargain

Sweet Nothings Bake Shop, Book 4

Kristen Dixon

THIGPEN-GANDY PUBLISHING

Thigpen-Gandy Publishing

Contents

ONE

Salon Faux Pas

SIENNA

I have a confession to make. I hate the salon. Okay, so, I don't *hate it* hate it, but the salon and I have a love-hate relationship. On-again, off-again? It's complicated. On the one hand, I get amazing colors there, and I love color. I *live* for color. Art is my passion. On the other . . . in this small town, the one and only salon is the biggest gossip mill this side of the Mississippi.

That's right. There's only one, in the whole town. Love the color, hate the chit-chat. It's not that I don't love the people, truly. Just about everybody in Adele is like family. That's the thing, though—there's just something *awkward* about being in a chair getting unicorn colors applied to the bottom third of your hair next to your third-grade teacher, who's really intent on finding out why you're still not married, and if so—would you like to date her brother?

Yeah, that's a big fat *no*.

Hence the complicated relationship with the salon.

If I was capable of giving up my beloved rainbow of hair colors, maybe it would have all gone down differently. *Maybe* I wouldn't have walked into the town gossip mill one fine Thursday afternoon and been roped into the most ridiculous matchmaking plot in this century, which led directly to me experiencing the heartbreak of my life. But I can't, and I did. It can only go up from here, right? *Right*?

Let me back up to the beginning.

My sister was going to be the death of me. Really, truly, the death of me. Or at least my career. Her last text was practically burned into my retinas, after the number of times I'd read it. Fury tended to have that effect on people. Even today, as I walked into my monthly salon appointment for a color touch-up, I could still see it dancing in front of me, mocking my latest attempt to make my flaky older sister grow up. Twelve *minutes* older than me, and never once did she let me forget it.

Suze: *S, won't make it to the office tomorrow. Something came up. *wink emoji* *heart eyes emoji* Cover for me, kay?*

I'd bet my last dollar that the s*omething* was a some*one* who had a set of rocking abs but no job, driver's license, or prospects.

Stuffing down my simmering rage, I shoved the glass door open a little too hard, the tinkling bell overhead reaching an unpleasant pitch with the force, and nearly knocking Mrs. Lindy's large tote bag over in the process. That earned me a scowl, and a tap on the toe with her cane.

"Young lady, what is your hurry? You nearly knocked my bag over!"

"Sorry, Mrs. Lindy. Bad day."

"Hmm." She pursed her lips and cast a speculative look up and down my outfit, back up to my hair. "Well, I don't see an emergency. Surely your mama taught you better?"

I sighed, tempted to just turn around and walk back out. I was off on the wrong foot, and I hadn't made it past the welcome mat. But the idea of Suzanne ruining my favorite monthly ritual on top of flaking on the job I'd stuck my neck out to get her? Nope, not happening. So, I fastened on my best apologetic smile, and made it right. *If only my slacker of a sister had ever managed to do the same.*

"I'm sorry, Mrs. Lindy, Suzanne just sent me an unpleasant message, and I took it out on the door. I didn't mean for you and your bag to get caught in the crossfire."

Her hawk-eyes softened, and she reached over and patted me on the hand, all trace of her earlier irritation gone in an instant. "Honey, you have got to give yourself a break where she's concerned. She's a wild one, that sister of yours. You have been runnin' behind her and cleanin' up her messes since you were six years old. That's a lot on one young lady's shoulders. Y'all are in your thirties. It's high time you let her sink or swim on her own. Whatever it is she's done now, *let it go*." With a gentle squeeze, she let me go.

I walked numbly to the reception desk to let Anna know I was here for my ritual color change, the words rattling around in my brain. Could I really ever just let it go? It didn't feel like it. Every family dinner, mama was after me to help Suzanne. Every month when rent came due, there was Suzanne, hand out. Every time she got into a scrape, I was the one getting the call at two a.m. for pickup. Jail?

Check. Side of the road motel? Check. Random truck stop in Tucson? That was a long drive, and check.

Frankly, the latest issue was salt in the wound. When I sat down to wait my turn in the chair, I didn't even pull out my phone and browse the latest art trends on my favorite app. I just sat mulling.

I was so lost in my own thoughts—and maybe imagining a hundred ways for my wayward sister to get her comeuppance—that I almost missed him.

Jenny Abernathy-Colee's youngest little one toddled over and banged my knee with her sippy cup, snapping me out of my distraction. "Oh, no-no, Miss Emma. You better go on back to mama."

"Sorry, Sienna!" Jenny hustled over with her cape flapping and scooped up the wayward child, planting a big kiss on her round little cheek. "She's learned to walk, and now we can't stop her. You were supposed to stay next to mama's chair, Emma," she scolded slightly as she hustled back to Evangeline, who was waiting with the scissors to finish her haircut.

I smirked, knowing Emma would be back in two seconds flat, and scanned the salon for any other possible assailants. I didn't mind; the kids around here were just about everybody's. We all lent a hand when needed, and nobody thought twice about it. It was odd, though, watching my friends all grown up and having babies, while I was still single and living alone. I'd always thought I'd be right there with them, but my job was so demanding I hadn't taken the time to really look for *Mister Right* like I should.

Plus, the few dates I'd had with people I'd met at work leaned more towards the side of Mister *Always* Right. No thanks.

I watched as Emma toddled off, instead of heading for me, heading towards the back of the salon where there were more booths behind a mirrored divider and also the storage racks full of extra product. Jenny closed her eyes and sighed and was about to heave herself out of the chair yet again when I waved her off.

"I'll get Emma, you just get your hair cut."

She met my eyes, hers filled half with gratefulness half an apology. "Thank you, Sienna. What am I going to do with her?"

I winked at her. "Raise her right and let her loose on the world, obviously."

She chuckled, as Evangeline made quick work of her trim.

Walking around the divider to the back row of booths, I spotted Emma, making a beeline for one of the other hairdressers' purses, tucked away under the cabinets that held her styling tools.

"Emma, no, ma'am! Come to Aunt Sienna!" I clapped and sped up, hoping to intercept her before she delved into the sparkly handbag.

She giggled and toddled faster, her chubby little toddler legs making surprisingly good time, and allowing her to weave between spaces I had to turn sideways through.

"Emma!" I scooped her up under the arms just as her fingertips grazed the gem-studded fabric, letting out a triumphant, "Ha! Not today, miss priss!" I kissed the giggling toddler on the cheek and looked up to see an amused Finn Russell sitting in the stylist's chair for his haircut. "Oh, Finn, I'm sorry. I didn't even see you there."

He smiled, the action making the corner of his eyes crinkle distractingly. "It's okay, Sienna. You were on a mission. Good morning, Miss Emma."

He reached over and jiggled one of her shoes, making her kick and giggle harder, before stuffing her fingers in her drooly mouth. My arms tightened around her automatically, as my brain was on overdrive taking in the man mere inches from me. His brown hair was freshly trimmed, cropped close to his skin at the neck, and fading up into a tousled, longer thatch on top. It looked thick, and I was tempted with the sudden urge to run my fingers through it.

He pushed his glasses up his straight, perfectly proportioned nose and addressed Emma again. "Teething, huh?" he murmured, "I hear that's a rough business."

She burbled something around her fingers, and I realized I should probably say something. "Yep, she's just learned to walk. She's making the rounds and wanted to come for a visit." I smiled, forcing my eyes to stay on his face, and not travel down the plaid shirt, sleeves rolled up past his elbows, showing off toned forearms. But I *definitely* didn't notice that. Nope, not on Finn. *Absolutely not.*

He smiled up at me, then self-consciously reached up and touched his hair.

"Not sure about the cut?" I asked, sensing his uncertainty.

He shook his head, the faintest hint of a blush coloring his cheeks. "That obvious? Kat convinced me to try something new . . . what do you think?"

The woman in question emerged from the back, a tub of pomade clutched in her hand and a sway in her hips. "You'd better think it's fantastic, because *it is*. It was way past time to let go of the same haircut you've had since high school."

"It's definitely fantastic," I agreed. He pressed his lips together in embarrassment and looked down at his knees.

I couldn't help but follow the motion, and my eyes greedily drank in the sight of the well-worn denim clinging to his thighs. Quickly glancing back up at his face, I said with more sincerity, "I mean it, Finn. You're really attractive." His head jerked up, interrupting Kat who was slathering pomade into his thick hair and suddenly it clicked what I'd said. "Err, it is. The haircut is great. Ahh, yeah. Better take Emma back to her mom." I gave him and Kat an embarrassed nod and spun on my heel, quickly walking away. I'd shut the door on Finn a long, long time ago, and I had no interest in reopening it now.

Did I?

"Emma! There you are. Thank you, Sienna." Jenny smiled at me.

"No problem. It looks like Evangeline is almost done; why don't I let her sit with me?"

"That would be great."

I nodded, and carted Emma back to the waiting area of the salon, snagging a few of the children's books from the rack against the wall before I settled her on my lap. I held the book and started to read, but she was more interested in the colorful pictures, so I let her have free rein, flipping back and forth and cooing to her heart's content.

A minute later, Finn emerged from the back of the salon, his hair freshly styled and looking perfect, and the tub of pomade in his hand which he rolled back and forth nervously. Kat strolled at his side, his opposite in her ease as she chattered away.

"This is a simple style, and perfect for your time on the auction block. I know it's different, but trust me. You can pull this off. Let me know if you need outfit help for the big day; I've been dressing Cody for years." She patted his shoulder, before crossing behind the desk to cash him out. He nodded, but didn't respond to her offer of help to dress him.

I watched surreptitiously over Emma's head as he passed his card over to pay and let her bag up the pomade. He nodded to her, saying something quietly, then turned and waved at me before he strode out of the salon.

I waved back and tried my best not to watch him leave. We'd been friends as middle schoolers, but the friendship had died when we'd gone our separate ways for high school and college. He'd gone off to the nearest magnet school with a technology focus, while I'd been left behind until I could escape to my art program in college.

No sooner had the door clicked shut behind him than the talk started. I kept my head down, ignoring the chatter like I always did.

Missy was the first to jump in. "Can you believe Dolly convinced him to join the Bachelor auction?

I never thought I'd see the day; that one keeps to himself like it's a religion."

Mrs. Lindy snorted delicately; the sound somehow ladylike. "Have you ever known anyone to truly stand up to Dolly? She's a freight train in a floral blouse."

I had to resist the urge to chuckle at that; Finn's aunt Dolly really was something else.

"Y'all knock it off. Finn's a sweet boy," Kat interjected. "Maybe this auction will be a good thing. He's shy, and this will give him a chance to find the one."

Missy flipped her bleach-blonde hair over her shoulder and leaned in, fervor in her eyes. "I don't know, Cindy is on the war path after he broke it off with her. Do you really think anybody is going to bid? If I had to guess, he's going to be mighty lonely—and mighty humiliated—standing up there all alone. If it was George, they'd bid the town down. But Finn? He doesn't have many lady friends."

My mouth twisted in anger at the thought, and I had to bite my tongue not to say something. Why should she sound smug about Finn being more of a loner? He kept to himself, sure, but he'd always been quiet. He wasn't a bad guy just because he wasn't always trying to be the town star; we couldn't *all* be prom kings and queens, after all.

Jenny walked up, holding her hands out to Emma, who wiggled free of my lap, the book immediately abandoned in favor of her mama.

"Hey Jenny, what is this bachelor auction they're talking about?" I stood and asked quietly.

She rolled her eyes. "Oh, some new fundraiser. If you ask me, some of the mamas in this town are getting impatient. They want grandbabies, stat. The bachelor auction is just a ploy to get some new matches going around here. Why?"

"Nothing, I just overheard some things." I cut my eyes over her shoulder to where Missy and Kat were arguing over the checkout counter. "I hadn't heard about it, yet," I admitted.

"Oh yeah, I think they announced it while you were off at that art conference thingy." She waved, and I grimaced at the reminder of the very dull, very corporate conference I'd had to fly to Reno for. The lack of humidity was nice, but that was about all. "It's Saturday. You should come. Maybe pick up a hot date." She grinned, knowing how much I absolutely *did not* like to participate in the collective town shenanigans.

"That's about as likely as me shaving my head bald today," I groused.

She laughed and gave the wiggling Emma a grin. "That means it's not happening, Emma-girl. Let's get you home for a nap. Wave bye to Aunt Sienna."

Her chubby-fingered wave brought a smile to my lips, and I waved back as Jenny headed to pay.

Evangeline caught my attention. "You ready, Sienna? What are we doing today?" She bounced her shoulders excitedly. "Give me something interesting."

"Hmm, I'm thinking purple this month."

"Ooh, dark and mysterious purple, or light like cotton-candy purple?"

"Let's go for mysterious."

"I like it. Let's get you to my station and see what we can do." She ran her fingers through the ends of my hair, already speculating.

Two

Tee Ball

SIENNA

Saturday mornings used to be for sleeping in, but lately I was always up at the crack of dawn for one of my friends' kids' sports games. I didn't mind it, really, because I enjoyed the quiet early morning hours when the day was still full of opportunity. Checking the clock, I put my charcoal pencil down, and headed to the kitchen to wash my hands and get a travel mug of coffee ready.

Today was tee ball at the park, and frankly, it was adorable. After a quick peek in the mirror to admire my new cut and color, I headed off down the sidewalk. It was about two miles to the park, and the cool air would do me good. I needed some time to think, and after a quick puff of my inhaler, I set out.

Yesterday at work had been awful, and as my feet hit the pavement, one of my bosses' words echoed in my head.

"Your sister not showing up has really made the upper management team wonder about her commitment to the firm, and frankly, it doesn't look good for you, either. You recommended her. Do you think this firm can have its receptionists missing? We have important clients. They deserve to be treated with respect, and you need to respect the business that happens here."

As if I'd ever missed a day, a night of overtime, or complained about endless revisions from those oh-so-self-important clients? No. Not once. So, when my sister—who'd only worked there for two weeks, not seven years like I had—flaked, suddenly I was mud? It stung, but sadly I couldn't say I was surprised. Then, because that wasn't enough, I'd gotten caught in traffic and my normal forty-five minute commute had doubled.

My graphic design firm might sell what they called art, but there was no soul to the business. It was all deadlines and dollar signs, and my artistic heart hated every second. But, it was steady, and paid the bills. Ever since I was a kid, my mom had been drilling into me how important it was to be stable and take care of myself. Don't depend on anyone else. You can only trust yourself.

It made sense, looking back; my dad had walked out on her with twin toddlers, and she'd struggled to make it. She was the only person she could depend on, and from her perspective my desire to be an artist was a colossal mistake. So, I'd gone to school for graphic design; the closest I could get to art and still be useful in business.

It sucked. I wasn't free to make what I wanted; I was chained to my computer, spinning out endless revisions on corporate logos and document packages that were not much different from the ones before them. I wanted to create something exciting, something fresh. I wanted to make a living off of art that inspired me. I was paid well, though, and I'd never considered leaving. I had my own place, decent retirement savings, and no debt. So, I had achieved the all-important security my mom had drummed into my head . . . I was just miserable. And it's not like there was extra cash flying around. I had enough, and it was just that: enough. I used to dream of having my own shop, but that plan had been well and truly squashed over the years.

I passed through the entrance gates of the ball field, and my head wasn't any clearer. It would have to wait. I spotted Marlie and Jenny across the way, and beelined across to them. Marlie was sprawled in a hot pink folding camp chair, with her eyes closed, sweat-plastered hair, and a largely swollen belly. Tucker stood behind her, rubbing her shoulders as he watched the preschoolers run around the bases.

"No, buddy, wrong way," he murmured, and stopped rubbing one of her shoulders to wave the child the other way. "Hey, Sienna."

"Hey, Tucker. Ladies." Jenny waved but didn't stop bouncing baby Emma on her knee.

Jenny's husband John waved as well, without looking away from the action out on the field, as James, their oldest, grinned and dropped his hat. He stopped to pick it up, and then continued running back towards first base.

Marlie opened one eye and giggled as she watched her nephew round the bases in reverse, then looked up at me. "Hey girl, working on your art again this morning?"

"Uhm, yes?"

"You've got a smudge—" She gestured vaguely in the direction of my face.

I groaned. "Seriously? I passed like four people on the way over here and nobody said a word."

"Your reputation as the quirky artist type must be getting around, then."

"Sounds great," I responded drily as I used my phone camera to find the giant charcoal smudge across my cheekbone.

"Mm, could be worse. They could be calling you a cat lady. Oh, or a spinster. It's been a while since Mrs. Lindy's had a chance to call me that." She rubbed her belly happily. "But I'm sure she's willing to share the love with a new victim."

"At this rate, she's not far off."

"Oh, come on. Other than Jenny, it took us all a while to settle down. And I have a feeling you're next."

"Riiiight," I drawled, shoving my phone back into my pocket and looking back out at the field. "So, who's winning?"

"No idea," Jenny answered. "Sports remain a mystery to me, but I'm here and that has to count for something, right?"

"Ditto."

"So, what are you working on?" Marlie asked, eager to talk about anything besides tee ball. Tucker stopped rubbing and paced up to the chain-link fence to shout encouragement to James.

"What?" I asked, distracted by the fourteen preschoolers all converging on one base to try to catch a ball that kept rolling out of reach. "Are they supposed to do that?"

"You'll have to ask Tucker. I meant the art smudge. Is it a new project?" She reached down and picked up a giant to-go cup of tea from Jude's, eyes rolling back in bliss as she sipped.

"You and that tea need a minute alone?" Jenny and I chuckled, and she narrowed her eyes at me.

"One, yes we do. This icy goodness completes me. Two, don't ever let me be this pregnant in the summer again, because it's hot as Satan's back porch out here. And three, don't change the subject, you weird little art secret keeper. Why is every project so hush-hush?"

I shrugged, embarrassed by my superstitious ritual. "I don't know, Marlie. You know how it is. I can't talk about it until it's perfect. It's . . . coming along. That's all for now."

She sighed, but didn't argue. Jenny, however, took up the charge without missing a beat.

"Well, if you don't want to talk about art, what about the auction this afternoon? Are you going to head on down for some good old-fashioned love at the auction block? I feel like Garth Brooks would approve." She lowered her sunglasses and waggled her eyebrows suggestively at me. "We need to hurry up and find you a man, so you can join us on this joyous journey of motherhood."

"So joyous," Marlie muttered between sips of her tea. She was due in a month; I couldn't blame her for hating the heat.

"No way, no how, am I going to go bid on a man. That's the most ridiculous thing I've ever heard."

"Okay, fine, you can be a stick in the mud all you want, but haven't you heard who's going to be on the block?"

"Nope, and I don't need to," I said firmly.

"M'kay, but hear me out. Fergusons. Yes, you heard that right. *Multiple* Fergusons. Reclusive cowboy landowners? Those. Mark Bradenton. Lucas Evans and Pete Stockton, too. That is a *whole* lot of man to go around."

"Finn, too," I murmured, thinking out loud.

"What's that?" Marlie asked, eyes closed again.

"Nothing, just talking to myself." I felt a blush climbing up my neck.

"I'm just saying, it's time you took your love life as seriously as you do your work life. We aren't in a fairytale movie here, if we want happily ever after, we're going to have to do some of the legwork on our own."

"I don't know, I found mine at the grocery store. You already buy groceries, right?" Marlie yawned, and now it was Jenny's turn to roll her eyes to the heavens.

"Take a nap, Marlie. Here's my plan. The auction starts right before this game ends. Once the game finishes, we leave the kids with the men and skedaddle on over and hook you a Ferguson. My treat. I bet he'll take you out to the family ranch and feed you a home-cooked meal under the stars. A handsome man, a beautiful meal, all by moonlight. Doesn't that sound great?" She pinned me with a challenging stare.

"Okay, yes, a date under the stars does sound great."

"Don't forget the handsome man," Marlie interjected.

"But it's weird. Me bidding on him? Call me old-fashioned, I always assumed the guy would be doing the pursuing. Besides, how humiliating if I bid on a date, and then he doesn't like me in the least? At least if a man asks you out, you know they're into the idea. These poor guys have all been strong-armed into public humiliation for a sense of civic duty. Noble, sure, but it doesn't mean they're all on the marriage mart. This isn't the seventeen hundreds."

"Oh, come on. Don't take it that seriously. So what, if he's not the one? Sometimes, you need to dust yourself off and go out on a limb. Not because you think you're going to find the man of your dreams in one night at a kooky town gathering, but just to make yourself available. Have a conversation, talk about nothing, give love a chance. Maybe you'll be surprised."

I squinched my mouth to the side, equal parts horrified and intrigued. She was right, I was all work and no play. No *love*. And I didn't want to be the crazy art lady, alone in a house full of progressively weirder canvases for the rest of my days. It was just a lot.

"Fine, but I'm not making any promises. You two goons can go with me, and we'll just see what happens."

"That's what I'm talking about! Good decision."

Tucker let out a whoop of glee from the fence line, and we spotted one of the kids dashing for home plate. We all cheered, and for the moment, my love life was forgotten, just the way I liked it.

THREE

The Auction Block

SIENNA

The tee ball game ended, and despite my hopes that Jenny would drop it, I knew better. And so it was that less than an hour and a half later, the two of us scooped Marlie out of her camp chair, kissed the kids, and headed off arm-in-arm towards the firehouse, where the auction was being held. Apparently, the firemen had built an outdoor stage for the occasion. Dolly Blake was a frightening woman when she wanted to be.

We were still a block away when we heard the first cheers. Delia from the Charitable Matrons of Adele was up on the stage, and the crowd was eating up every word.

". . . and all of the money raised today will be staying right here, to repair damage from hurricane Darius last fall. Some of the families in our town are still recovering, and every single penny will be used to buy the supplies needed to get their homes back up to snuff. We all know insurance helps, but it certainly doesn't replace everything."

A murmur of agreement went through the crowd as we joined the back, and I felt guilty for so staunchly avoiding this. It was a good cause; I knew the Morgans in particular still had two rooms in their house closed and sheeted off with plastic because the insurance hadn't covered enough to get the whole house functional again. It sounded like more than one family was hurting in the same way.

Maybe I could help them and spend an enjoyable evening with a new guy. Where was the harm in that?

"We'll also be doing volunteer sign ups to do the labor, so we can stretch it to help all the families in need. Let's make our town whole again." Delia smiled warmly at the crowd and smoothed down the hem of her blouse.

The cheers this time reverberated off the old brick firehouse with deafening clarity, and without hesitation, she waved the first man up onto the stage.

"Hello, Mark. Thank you for being the first volunteer. Am I to understand you were also the first to sign up your talents to aid in the rebuilding efforts?"

Mark, looking more than a little nervous in his blue button-down, nodded and swallowed before answering into the outstretched microphone. "Yes, ma'am."

"Well, ladies, he has a giving heart. Isn't that something? Let's start the bidding for a date with Mark! What do you say, Mark, fifty dollars?"

He shrugged and stuffed his hands in his pockets nervously.

"Well now, sugar, don't be shy. We're all friends here, right? And soon, you'll be dating one of these fine ladies, so speak up!" As Delia kept talking, I scanned the crowd to see how many women were here to bid. A cluster of waitresses from Jude's—still in uniform—stood to one side of the crowd; Missy and her singles mixer set were all present; plus several others. It was a good turnout of the town's single ladies, and I was surprised. In fact, if Marlie and Jenny hadn't dragged me here, I might have been the only single woman not present.

Denise was the first one to wave her hand to bid on a date with Mark, and after that things moved quickly. Delia was in her element, talking faster and faster as bidding for Mark's date drew to a close at a respectable one hundred and twenty-five dollars. He waved to Stacy—the winner—in the crowd and ambled off to the side with a crooked grin on his face.

A quick look at Denise showed she was not happy to be outbid, but Stacy was beaming as she crossed to stand next to Mark; maybe love was in the air, after all.

Delia called out the next bachelor—one of the Ferguson brothers, looking unhappy to be there—and before she'd finished her introduction, Missy Jones had already hollered out an opening bid.

"Seventy-five!" she crowed, pulling a chuckle from the crowd.

Ashley from Jude's called out next, "Ninety!" and earned a glare from Missy for her troubles.

"Ooh, this is more fun than I thought it would be!" Marlie leaned heavily into my side, clutching my forearm. "Are you going to start bidding soon? I don't know how many bachelors there are to go around, and this crowd is *hungry*. Look at Missy, she's about to tear up anyone else who gets between her and a Ferguson."

Jenny cackled with glee and pulled a baggie of Teddy Grahams from her pocket. She pulled out a handful before offering the bag to me and Marlie.

"Not that kind of hungry, but thank you." I waved the bag away.

Marlie noshed her own handful down happily as Scott Ferguson was matched to a smug-looking Missy. She sauntered across the crowd, eyes boring holes in the man's broad shoulders as he stepped down from the stage. He'd no sooner made it to the bottom step than she had her arm looped through his, the pained expression on his face completely ignored as she hauled him off to the side.

After that, there was no more drama. Man after man was led across the stage, and dates were sold with surprising speed. I even saw a few pretty blushes from ladies in the crowd, enough to make me wonder if this was an opportunity many of them were glad for. Unlike me, who still didn't know why the heck I was here. Besides making my friends happy, of course. Marlie watched the proceedings with the glee of a mid-day soap opera, and the Teddy Grahams were long gone by the time Finn walked out onto the stage.

I could tell right off the bat he was nervous, and he ran a hand through his new haircut, jostling Kat's carefully-applied pomade. He scanned the now much thinner crowd—though some who'd already secured a match stood by, waiting to see how it all played out in the end.

"Hello, Finn. Lovely of you to agree to join us today. It is such a good cause, and I know you've got a good heart. And what a haircut! Am I right ladies?"

There was a small murmur of approval from the crowd and a smattering of claps from the bored men who'd already paid their dues, but the energy had died down somewhat, and my stomach tightened. Was Missy right? Was Finn about to be humiliated in front of half the town?

"This is not Finn's first foray into charity, as he's a regular donor to the humane society—have you seen their new website? That was Finn!—and also teaches technology classes at the senior center once a month, helping to set up their ereaders, new cell phones, and any other assistance they might need to be *hip to the times*," Delia joked, clapping Finn on the back.

He gave her a nervous grimace in lieu of a smile before looking down at the boards under his feet, probably wishing they'd swallow him up. In that moment, a sense of calm resolve washed over me. I might be no damsel in shining armor, but Finn was a nice guy—he kept to himself like me, and no he wasn't the most popular guy in town by a long stretch—but he had been my friend back in middle school. He wasn't going to go down without a bid. Not today, not on my watch.

"All right then, let's start the bidding at fifty dollars. Do we have any takers?" Delia scanned the crowd, and I waited a second to see if anyone else was planning to bid. After a long beat of silence, I threw my hand up in the air.

"Oh, wonderful. We have fifty. Sixty?" Finn's shoulders straightened and his head snapped up, scanning the crowd to see who'd bid, but I'd already lowered my hand.

I held my breath, waiting to see if I'd be contested, and ignored my best friends gaping openly at my side.

"Going once, going twice—" Delia looked expectantly around, but no more hands were lifted for Finn. "One date with Finn, sold for fifty dollars! You got a steal!" She clapped encouragingly and shooed a grateful Finn from the stage.

"You just bought a date. Oh, my *gawd*, do you have a crush on Finn? You haven't breathed a word about him since school! I never dreamed—"

"Jenny," I hissed under my breath, making pointed eyes at the crowd we were standing behind, "not now, okay?"

"You owe us details later. Go get your man!" Marlie half-squealed, drawing more eyes our way as I slowly wove through the crowd, to where Finn waited at the bottom of the steps.

The moment his eyes locked on mine, I saw surprise and something I couldn't name cross his features, but his face quickly morphed into a friendly smile.

"Sienna, wow! I didn't see you coming . . . literally, *or* metaphorically." He jammed one hand in his back pocket and tried to run the other through his styled hair, promptly knocking a piece free of its place.

"Shocking, given my purple hair." I returned his smile and nodded over to the side, where the other freshly minted couples loitered.

He laughed, the genuine sound doing something to my stomach, and followed me to the open area past the other couples, chatting and probably making date plans.

"So, I guess this means we're going on a date, huh?" He smiled half-way, and I would swear I detected anxiety underneath his cool façade.

"That's the idea," I murmured, searching his face for clues.

"If you want to, of course. This was a charity thing, so, if you don't actually want to go—"

That misplaced hair was distracting me from his ramble, so I reached up and gently tucked it back where it belonged, swooped up with its brothers. My fingers itched to linger, but I slowly pulled them back and met his eyes again. "That's better. What were you saying?"

"Uhm—" His gaze locked on my fingers, hovering between us like they were going to go back for round two. "I was asking what night was good for you? I can make any evening work that's convenient."

"Hmm, I have a late meeting on Tuesdays, but otherwise my evenings are free."

"Okay, not Tuesday. This might sound weird, but is it okay if I check the weather and text you with a day?"

"I guess so . . . afraid of the rain?" I chuckled, imagining a southerner afraid of rain. Though, he was a notorious lover of electronics, so I supposed they wouldn't appreciate spring and summer showers.

"No, no. I just have something specific in mind, and I don't want anything to ruin it. You deserve the best."

This time his smile was the one I remembered, crooked, with a hint of straight white teeth peeking through and the tiniest hint of dimple on the right side. My stomach did a backflip that I wasn't expecting, and I did my best to keep my face from showing it. This was a charity thing, after all. Rebuilding after a storm. Sad, broken houses getting repaired.

Yep, I could tell myself that until the sun came up tomorrow, and it wouldn't change a single thing; my pulse was racing, my stomach was full of butterflies, and I knew with absolute certainty that I wanted to get my hands back into his hair.

It was even softer than I'd suspected.

"Well then, you just let me know. You still have my number?" I asked, my voice coming out lower than usual, the sultry sound reflecting my thoughts.

He swallowed slowly, then nodded. "Yes, ma'am."

I rolled my eyes at his unnecessary formality and bumped his shoulder with mine. The brief contact sent a frisson of warmth bolting down my arm, making my fingertips tingle. "Okay then, let's talk soon."

"Absolutely."

With one last smile in his direction, I turned and started walking back to the house. I would swear on my mama's corn casserole that I felt his eyes follow my every step.

A while later, I let myself into my front door and abandoned my coffee cup in the sink, before grabbing a cold glass of water. Water in hand, I crossed to my art station, and cleared the charcoal project I'd been perfecting this morning off to the side. Somehow, I'd lost interest in it.

As I pulled a fresh, clean canvas from the bin below my table, I debated where to start. I picked up a tube of paint and a clean palette, envisioning a pair of warm hazelnut eyes with crinkles at the corners and the signature glasses that framed them. I bit my lip and started to paint.

FOUR

The Grind

SIENNA

Monday found me sitting in my cubicle, distractedly adjusting the color palette on my latest project to match the client's exact logo shades. It was a minimalistic piece, but it was meant to be the foundation of their new branding package, and with it they would get a full write up of all the shades, fonts, and images they could use across their product line and storefronts. It was very important, and yet I hadn't the least bit of interest in it.

Don't get me wrong, I had done my job well, and I knew they would be pleased with the end result. The palm tree curved into the S on their name just

so, and the colors were cool while still being profes-
sional. Very business tropical, which was the brief.

It was just . . . not where my heart was these days.
In my mind, I saw the empty storefront by the lake
on Oak Street, and imagined hanging my canvases there, and selling art supplies between teaching
mixed media classes to eager kids, and adults, too.
With a sigh, I saved the file and submitted it to the
team's work board. I watched the little green check
mark appear, which was meant to be encouraging.
So, why didn't I feel it? I picked up my coffee mug
to find it empty, of course. I swung my chair back,
but the unexpected buzz of my cell stopped me from
getting up and heading straight for caffeine.

*Finn: Hi, Sienna. I hope the rest of your weekend
was great. If you're still open, Thursday night is going
to have the best weather for what I have planned. Can
I pick you up at 6:30?*

*Sienna: Thursday sounds good. Do I get to know
what the plan is, or is it a surprise?*

Finn: . . .

. . .

*Well, I can tell you if you want. But I was going to
keep it a surprise.*

*Sienna: Okay, just a wardrobe hint, then. What
should I wear?*

Finn: Oh, well. I'm not an expert at women's fashion. Hmm.

I chuckled, imagining his scrunched-up face perfectly as he thought it over.

"Well, isn't this a surprise. You're rarely smiling these days. What's gotten into you, Sienna?"

I bit down a sigh that wanted to escape at Bryan's voice, bursting my happy bubble as he crowded into the entry of my cubicle.

"Is it a crime to smile here, now?" I looked up and arched an eyebrow at him in challenge.

"Of course not! The rest of us do it regularly. You're usually just more . . . reserved," he said the word like it was a mark against me instead of a sign that I kept to myself and did my work, which was the truth. I just wasn't in his boys' club, and he hated that I got half of the top clients, just like him, when he'd been there two years longer.

"Maybe I'm just reserved around you, Bryan. Excuse me, I was just heading for some coffee."

He didn't leave, instead stepping just far enough to the side so that I had to brush past him to get out. *Jerk.*

I hadn't gone three steps before he followed me, and I ground my teeth together.

"I saw you finished with the PTP. Was that the last thing in your work queue? I hear there's a new client

36

being announced at the meeting this afternoon. A big one." He caught up to me, keeping pace at my shoulder as I did my best to portray through pointed silence my utter disinterest in talking to him.

"There usually is if they move the weekly meeting to announce it," I murmured, since he clearly wasn't going to drop it.

"Yeah, the question is, are you going to put your name in the hat?" We reached the break room and he stepped ahead of me, pressing his palm flat against the door as if to open it, but stalling.

"Bryan, you know it doesn't matter who puts their name where. Tim is going to assign it to whoever's artistic style is the best fit for the client directive. Period. Now move, please, you're blocking me from the coffee." I shooed him aside with my mug, and he narrowed his eyes, but pushed the door open and held it for me. I walked past him and beelined to the coffee maker, picking a pod from the little carousel of options. I reached for my usual dark roast and stopped, spotting a hazelnut blend. *Hazelnut, like the eyes in her painting.*

The corner of my mouth twitched up of its own accord as I changed course and popped the new flavor into the machine.

"See, you're smiling again. This isn't a joke, Sienna." I jumped at his words, as I hadn't realized he'd followed me into the breakroom. He continued on, completely oblivious to my discomfort. "Are you going after the new client, or not? I don't know if you know this, but I'm in line for assistant art director for our entire floor. I want it, and I don't want you getting ideas and getting in my way. I've paid my dues, Sienna. I've *earned* this."

I spun, my anger simmering close to the surface, now. "Then what are you so afraid of, Bryan? If you've *earned this*, then you'll get it. And if you don't, well, I guess you haven't earned *jack*, now, have you?" The machine behind me began to pour its delicious nectar into my cup, and I pointed him toward the break room door. "Now, if you'll excuse me, I've *earned* five minutes alone with my coffee."

He snorted in irritation and stormed out, letting the door shut a little too hard behind him. *And he wonders why I never smile when he's around.* I sighed and leaned my hip against the countertop as the coffee maker finished.

My phone buzzed in my pocket, and I fished it out to see if Finn had finally decided what the appropriate outfit was for our date. When the screen unlocked, I saw four messages queued.

Finn: Really, whatever you're comfortable in is fine.
Finn: But let's call it casual.

Finn: I mean, still fun, and date-like. I don't want you to think it's casual, casual. Nice casual?

Finn: I absolutely have a plan, I promise.

I grinned, and quickly tapped out a return message.

Sienna: Sounds perfect. I think I have just the right sundress for the job. *wink emoji*

Finn: Well then, I think you're set. See you Thursday.

Sienna: See you Thursday.

Just as I was about to slip it back into my pocket and sugar up my coffee, it buzzed again.

Finn: Thank you for bidding on me, Sienna.

I didn't respond, unsure how to answer that. Instead, I stirred a few packets of sugar into my coffee, and took my first sip.

The hazelnut was different, but in a good way. It was new and different, and it brought a smile to my face, just like a certain man I knew.

I had a few minutes left before the afternoon meeting, and I spent it straightening my desk. Mid-scoop of a bunch of mangled paperclips into the trash can, my one friend at the office, Tamika, poked her head into my cubicle. Her mass of curly hair bounced to a stop a moment after she did.

"Girl, did I hear correctly that you went to the town nut-fest and bought yourself a man at auction? Tell me that is not the real headline."

A strangled laugh-turned-groan escaped my throat as I tried to think of how to explain. "Okay, one, you're not from around here, so don't judge. Two, no, I did not *buy a man*, I donated to hurricane relief by way of . . . a date." I waved my hand, as if to brush it all aside. "No big deal."

"Uhm, yes it is. You haven't dated anyone since . . . what was his name? Big teeth guy?" She gestured to her top lip, and I dropped my head into my hands.

"Tamika, Dirk was a nice guy!"

"Uh huh, real nice. And somewhere in his family tree was a beaver. What's the charity-date look like? Got a picture?" She scooted into my cubicle and leaned her hip against my desk, clearly not willing to drop it.

"I could probably find one," I admitted, thoughts of a squeaky-clean desk forgotten in lieu of girl talk.

"You do that. Did I see Bryan chase you into the break room earlier? He is a pit bull, that one."

"Yes, don't remind me. He's up in arms about whatever new client is getting announced today."

She rolled her eyes. "Ooh, yeah. Word's spread that he's gunning for the assistant art director position. As if we need him to have a title with *director* in it." She fake coughed, "Dictator."

I snorted at her ridiculous humor, and she grinned at me. "So, where's my picture?"

"Oh, sorry. Hang on." I quickly pulled up a social media site and scrolled until I found him. His profile picture was cute, but dated, so I scrolled until I saw where he'd been tagged in a photo of his best friend's wedding. I enlarged the photo and held up my phone to show Tamika.

"Girl, where can I donate to this hurricane relief? Because he's the best kind of geek-chic I've ever seen." She fanned herself and leaned in to take Finn in a little closer. "He's got kind eyes, *and* a jawline I'd like to see up close and personal."

I blushed, thinking of the painting sitting partially complete on my easel at home. "He's a really sweet guy, actually."

She looked up from my phone, and I could see the questions written on her face. "Sweet? Don't tell me you've friend-zoned him. That would be stupid, Si-si. This man needs to be walked right out of friend-zone and right into, 'hello sir would you like to father smart babies with me' zone." She jiggled her shoulders like she was dancing, and then added,

"He is smart, right? He looks smart. Those glasses? Perfection."

"Yes, he's incredibly intelligent."

"Incredibly, huh? Ooh, you *do* like him. How did I not know this? I have been remiss."

"No, it's just . . . I've known him forever, but we don't run into each other often. Neither of us is the type—"

"Don't try to tell me he's not your type. Because if you do, he's going to be really surprised when I show up on his date instead. He's *my* type."

Was that what I was doing? Was I trying to build up obstacles, before we'd even gone on a date? *Friend-zone* him? I was too stubborn to admit that she might have a point.

"Okay, give me a little credit here. I wasn't going to say he's not my type. I was going to say neither of us are the type to rock the boat. When you've known someone forever and haven't been close since before college . . . going on a date is rocking the boat." *The safe, distant boat.*

She snorted, and repressed a giggle behind her hand, shoulders shaking.

"What? What's so funny?"

She whispered a little too loud, "If the boat's a-rockin', don't come a-knockin'!"

"Oh, my word, *Tamika!*" I clapped a hand over my mouth, too, to stifle a mortified giggle. "That is *not* what I meant."

She straightened, suddenly serious. "Oh, the pit bull pack is headed into the conference room. We better go find seats before they pee all over the place."

"You are crazy, girl, but I love you."

"Of course, you do; I am spectacular." She whipped her hair around and propped a hand on her hip as she waited for me to gather my notebook and a pen.

"You keep me sane."

She shot me a wink, and then led the way to the conference room, bowling through the cluster of Bryan and his cronies without missing a beat.

"'Scuse us, coming through." She sashayed in and grabbed a seat at the middle of the conference table, only a few seats from the head of the table where Randy always sat to lead the meetings. I sat next to her, and within moments the entire creative department had poured in—a full house for the announcement.

Randy was the last one in, and he shut the door before taking his usual seat. "Good afternoon, everyone. We'll make this quick since it's outside of the usual schedule, but I wanted to get everyone together to announce a new client. They're high profile and are expecting a lot of media coverage in their launch year. As such, they've come to us as well as two other firms, requesting pitches before selecting who they want to continue with. It's not our usual business model, however, for a business this big we're making an exception." He paused, looking around the table for questions. When none arose, he continued on.

"Now, they're operating on a tight timeline for this first phase because they want to have a design firm under contract within one week so they can get a full branding workup before their launch next month. Because of the tight deadline, we're going to do something a bit different," he said, gazing around the room. My eyes followed, and I saw that Bryan was leaning forward expectantly.

"We're going to have a good old-fashioned design contest. If you're working on a project, that's fine. We still need to meet existing deadlines. However, if you have any free time whatsoever, I'd like to encourage you to direct it towards this. Everyone has an equal opportunity here, and we're going to pitch the top five to the client. If they choose your pitch, we're offering a five-thousand-dollar bonus."

With that promise still hanging in the air, he flipped open his leather portfolio and gave each of us a handout, listing the client's creative brief. It was a simple, bullet-pointed list with a company name at the bottom. I scanned it quickly, my mind already whirring with the possibilities.

Once everyone had received their brief, Randy stood, readying to leave. "Let's make it spectacular, folks. I want their business, and you should, too. The presentations are due on my desk Monday at noon." With a nod, he strode from the room, and murmurs broke out like goosebumps in his wake.

"Five grand? Man, I could do a lot with that." Tamika shook my arm excitedly. "What about you? Are you going to submit a pitch? Of course you are—I mean, why not?"

My mind went immediately to that empty storefront over on Oak Street, just begging to be filled with life, and color. Five thousand dollars could pay first and last month's rent, maybe more if I could negotiate with the owner. Could this client bonus make my dream a reality?

"Yeah, Tamika, I'm going to submit a pitch."

"We're going to crush this thing." She grinned as we both stood and trailed the rest of our team out of the room. I was already so lost in idea mode I almost missed the glare Bryan shot over his shoulder at me on the way out.

FIVE

Work In Progress

SIENNA

The next few days passed in a blur of work, home, and sleep. I thought about texting Finn a time or two, but didn't want to seem too eager. Instead, when I kicked my heels off at the door and shrugged out of my work blouse, I always ended up back in front of my easel in a ratty t-shirt, brush in hand, bringing to life the next piece of the puzzle on the canvas. The human face was complex, and to show personality you really had to perfect the layering.

I was highlighting a cheekbone Wednesday evening when my phone buzzed. I ignored it, lost as

I was in the play of the light, until it buzzed again. And again.

With a sigh, I set down my brush.

The top message was from my sister, who was still MIA from work.

Suze: *Si, what's this I hear about a five-large bonus? Why didn't you tell me? I could use some extra cheddar right about now.*

My jaw dropped in irritation. Was she serious right now?

Sienna: *Are you kidding me? If you need money, COME TO WORK. Besides, you're not in the art department. How did you even hear about it?*

Suze: *From Renee. It certainly wasn't from my *loving* sister. Maybe I'd come to work if you thought I was worth more than being a SECRETARY. I have just as much talent as you, and you know it.*

I angrily closed the text. That had been her argument our whole lives. She had every bit as much raw talent as me, so why did I "get all the good stuff." The honest to God truth was, she *was* talented. Maybe more than me. But Suzanne never applied herself. She had a short attention span, and never followed through if things got challenging.

The day I got accepted into the art program at UGA, she threw a fit and slammed out of the house. She'd never even applied, but she still couldn't handle that I'd gotten accepted for something she considered herself better at. Mom had been worried sick and on the verge of calling the police to report her missing two days later when she finally answered her phone call and agreed to come home.

I took a few deep breaths to put her out of my head and checked the next message. It was from Finn.

Finn: I've been thinking about our date all day. Can't wait to see you tomorrow.

I paused, unsure what to say. I had been stuck on an idea for the pitch, and had only four days left to perfect something if I wanted to put my name in the hat. It was my big chance at the money I needed to open my own art studio.

I had briefly considered asking him to postpone a week, until after the pitch, but that seemed rude. Deep down, I didn't want to discourage him. He was a really nice guy, and we used to have so much in common. Palms sweating, I texted back.

Sienna: Can't wait to see you, too. Curious to find out what this plan of yours is.

*Finn: Good things come to those who wait. *Wink emoji**

*Sienna: I guess we'll find out tomorrow, won't we? *Wink emoji**

I set my phone down, flipping it to silent, and picked up the brush again.

Thursday at work seemed to drag, as I stared at my screen, waiting for inspiration to strike. The problem was, it wasn't. Unless I wanted to work all weekend, I only had today and tomorrow to design the presentation. I checked the clock on my computer for the hundredth time, and it finally read four o'clock. Time to go home and get ready for my date. The project in front of me, unfortunately, was still nothing but a blank background with some generic texts, and a few font selections. Nothing inspired, and certainly nothing that was going to win me the new client, and the fat five-thousand-dollar bonus.

With a sigh, I shut down and packed up for the night. It had been like this a few times over the years, but mostly clients gave a very detailed brief with exactly what they wanted. This company hadn't given us much: a blank page in black and white, and carte blanche to do what we wanted for the pitch. It was a designer's dream—one we were rarely afforded—and yet . . . nada.

As I walked out the door of the office, I forced myself to switch gears, and do my best to get into a dating kind of mood. Finn was a sweet guy, and he didn't deserve to get all my work drama hauled along on the date. Blowing out a breath, I headed to my car, and hopefully to a nice evening with an old friend. Scratch that, Tamika was right.

I was going on a date with a handsome, intelligent man, and I was dang sure going to enjoy it; blocked at work or no.

Six twenty-seven found me bouncing on the balls of my feet, anxiously dabbing paint off my fingertips. My easel was angled toward the window to catch the evening sun, and I was studiously pretending not to watch the clock. My bright red heels lay on their sides next to my art station, the perfect complement to my blue lace sundress. I set aside the cleanup rag and bent down to slip them on right as a knock sounded at the door. He was punctual, always a good sign.

The second heel fought me, so I called out, "Just a second!" and hop-hobbled towards the door until it finally slipped into place. I arrived at the door out of breath and with my hair askew, but I made it.

Shoving stray purple locks behind my ear, I swung the door open to find Finn standing there looking breathtakingly handsome, a bouquet of flowers in his fist.

He wore a blue blazer over an artfully faded t-shirt and jeans. The blazer molded to his upper arms and shoulders perfectly to show off a hint of muscle, and the way his jeans fit should have been a crime.

"Hi, Finn!"

"Hello, Sienna. You look lovely this evening." He kept his eyes locked on mine, and I felt a simmer of heat start low in my belly.

"Thank you. You look fantastic yourself." He nervously adjusted his glasses, the frames highlighting his sharp cheekbones in a way that had become familiar again over the past week.

"These are for you," he murmured, gravel in his tone as he handed me the beautiful flowers. While some men might have gone with simple red roses, he'd gone with a riot of colors, as if he knew that's what I'd prefer. It sparked happiness somewhere deep down that he'd gone beyond the basic, even if this date was a big ol' town setup.

"They're perfect, thank you." I looked up again, and he gave me the most tentative of smiles. "I should put these in water. Do you want to come in for a minute?"

"Sure." He smiled and followed me inside. My heels clacked on the kitchen tile as I hunted up a vase, and he wandered toward the living room.

"Did you draw all of these?" His voice from the hallway was muffled by the water running, so I wasn't sure which he was asking about.

"Not all of them; a few I've bought at markets because they inspired me."

He chuckled. "I like the nose, it's cute."

"Thank you, I did that one. There's this dog down at the library—"

"Oh, it's Muffin! It looks exactly like him, the way he's always putting his nose up on the desk." His voice came closer to the end of the hall, as I plucked the flower stems out of the beribboned wrapper and tucked them into the glass vase.

"Yeah, it just hit me as funny, one day, and I started sketching it. It needed color, though, so I came home and painted him. The angle was hard, but I liked the end result."

"What about this one, the bench? What's the story there?" Flowers situated, I walked out of the kitchen and came around to the hall, so I could stand next to him and look at the pencil drawing of the bench. He had his head cocked to the side, really studying it, and I wanted to hug the stuffing out of him.

Not many people took my art seriously, and it meant something to me that he did.

"Mm, it's not so happy as Muffin. It looked lonely, sitting empty there in the rain. Something about it resonated with me, so I drew it." I shrugged, not sure what to say about me taking time to capture an empty, wooden bench from the edge of town.

He lifted up a finger and traced along the more worn edge and trailed it down to a divot on the paper, which I'd only partially disguised with a tuft of grass by the leg. "Is this a raindrop?"

"Yeah, it is."

"It's beautiful. Sad, in a way." His voice was soft, and I didn't know what to say, so I didn't. "Can you show me the rest? You've got so much cool stuff on the walls, mine are pretty bare by comparison." He gave me a lopsided grin, and it was infectious.

We spent the next few minutes working our way down the hall, and to each room with a piece hanging in it. After I'd shown him the painting of the bowl of lemons hanging in the kitchen—he spotted my easel.

"Are you working on one now? Can I see it?" He took two strides across the room as I froze in panic.

"No! Wait—" I gasped. He paused and turned halfway around to face me, a look of surprise on his face. "I—I don't share works in progress. I'm sorry, no one is allowed to see it until it's complete." *Or ever, in this case.* My cheeks heated, imagining his reaction upon seeing an unfinished rendering of *himself* on my easel before our first date. The man had

"Oh, okay. No problem." He gave me a smile, but it lacked the easy familiarity we'd had when he first arrived.

"Really, it's not you. Jenny and Marlie are forever giving me a hard time about it. I guess I'm superstitious. I want it perfect first, before anyone sees it." I ran a hand through my hair, the short purple locks a poor recipient for my sudden onset fluster.

"You don't owe me any explanation. It's your work. I get it, it would be weird if someone stood over my shoulder and asked questions while I was coding something. The end product is where it all makes sense." He took a few steps away from the corner with my work in progress, meeting me in the middle of the room.

"I bet," I agreed, tilting my head back to look up at him.

"Are you ready to head to the date?"

"Sure, I'll grab my purse." I smiled again before heading to the foyer, yet I couldn't help feeling that I'd put us on shaky footing by freaking out about the painting. I slid my purse strap over my shoulder, blowing out a silent breath as I led the way to the front door, grabbing the keys off a hook to lock up behind us.

Six

Sunsets & Sweet Lemonade

SIENNA

F inn held the door for me and drove us towards the edge of town. After a few minutes of chit chat, my curiosity got the better of me. "Is there . . . a restaurant this way? We're pretty close to the edge of town, and the only things I know of out this way are a couple farms, empty land, and well, the overlook. But no food. Although, I guess you didn't *specify* that the surprise involved food, I did assume—"

He cut me off with a gentle touch on my forearm. "I'm going to feed you, I promise, Sienna. I wondered when you'd guess—I never spent much time out here myself, but I presumed you would have, ahh . . ." He trailed off, looking sheepish.

Realization washed over me, and I had to bite back a laugh. "Are we— I mean, are you taking us to the overlook? AKA the town make out spot?"

The faintest hint of pink tinted his cheeks, and I tried to hold back the laugh that was bubbling up, but it squeaked out. It started as a single giggle, then snowballed into a racking, belly laugh. Somewhere along the way, he joined in. In a minute, I wiped tears from the corners of my eyes, and leaned my head to the side to look at him. "Is that a hint about where the evening's going? Because, frankly, I was not expecting that." I chuckled again.

"No! No, I mean—I would love to kiss you, of course; I'd be an idiot not to, but, uh, well . . . there are very limited options in town, and I know half the guys before the auction were arranging dates at Jude's, or that nice place at the edge of Savannah. I don't know, it felt impersonal to go to the same old spot that everybody goes."

I snorted. "So, you thought we'd go to the place all the *teenagers* go?"

Finn threw his head back against the seat, briefly looking up at the top of the truck before meeting my eyes again. "Look, I know it seems weird, but I promise it won't be weird. Trust me? Give me five minutes, and if you think it's stupid I'll turn around and drive you straight to Savannah."

Intrigued, I nodded. "I'm down. Whatever you've got planned, I'd like to see it. I'm sorry I laughed, it's just, when you started implying I'd been there before, I lost it. I'm flattered, though, that you would think someone wanted to take me there."

He took one hand off the wheel and rubbed his chin, the motion bringing attention to his clean-cut jawline, and I swallowed before looking away. "I don't know what to say to that. You've always been beautiful—heck, I was half in love with you back then—so yes, I did assume you'd probably been before. I admit, I was hoping for some nostalgia." He glanced over quickly to gauge my reaction—whether to the confession or the nostalgia, I didn't know. I *did* know I was flabbergasted by the admission. The shock must have shown plain as day on my face because he continued, "What? What is it?"

"You had a crush on me in school?"

"Yep, you were the whole package. Smart and pretty. Not to mention, brave in a way I could never be. You knew exactly what you wanted, and nothing was ever going to stop you from going after it. I admired that. Still do." He gazed out the window, lost in memories as we pulled off on the dirt road to the overlook.

I sat in stunned silence as we bumped down the pitted road, even though he drove carefully. That's what he thought? That I was brave? I didn't feel it, not anymore. The responsibilities of adulthood had taken their toll on me, and most days I felt stuck. I hadn't felt *brave* since the day I'd left for college. Could I be the girl he remembered again? The girl I remembered?

The road split and he took the left fork, heading up the grassy path to the top of the hill. It didn't take long before we reached the top, and he slid the shifter into park.

"Ready? It's almost time."

"Yep," I answered. "Time for what, exactly?" I asked when he opened my door and offered me a hand down. I slipped my hand in his, the heat from our palms sending an undeniable shiver through me.

"You'll see. Come on!" Excitement lit his tone, and he didn't let go of my hand as he grabbed a small cooler bag from the bed of the truck and headed toward the edge of the overlook. He was efficient, pulling out a thin quilt from a side pocket and spreading it out for us to sit on, and then opening the cooler.

"I thought this would be better with appetizers. I hope you still like chocolate," he murmured, reaching into the cooler and pulling out a Sweet Nothings bakery box. When he popped the lid, the deliciously intermingled scents of chocolate and fruit hit me, and he placed the box full of chocolate covered strawberries between us on the blanket. Next were two bottles of lemonade, tiny meatball sliders, perfect tiny cups of pasta salad, and a few electric candles, which he set out along each side of the blanket.

"This is . . . unexpected. And perfect." I looked out over the swimming hole below us, the end of the ancient rope swing trailing along the glassy surface.

"I'm glad you think so. I've always thought the sunset here would be something worth seeing. Especially with good company." He smiled, crinkling the corners of his eyes, and I felt drawn into him like a magnet. The brief tension between us earlier was long forgotten, replaced instead by a bubbling happiness in my chest.

"You think I'm good company? Even if I'm not the same brave girl you remember?" I asked, hating the edge of uncertainty in my voice.

"You'll always be the brave girl I remember. In sixth grade, I was so nervous about being on stage for the spelling bee I was ready to throw up. And you took me by the hand and led me to my seat. You refused to move to where you were supposed to sit, even when one of the teachers threatened to not let you participate. You had this stubborn look on your face, and you stared her down and said, "I'm not leaving my friend. He's scared.""

I blew out a shaky breath, and my eyes dropped to where my fingers played with a blade of grass poking over the edge of the blue quilt. "I don't feel it—not anymore. I had such big dreams, you know? And not many of them came to be."

He frowned and reached forward, trailing a finger along my cheek, the touch so soft I might have imagined it. "Tell me about them."

"It's silly, really. I've got nothing to complain about." I waved a hand, dismissing the question.

"It's not silly, not at all. Dreams are important. What's that saying— 'Where there is no hope, the people perish?'"

I smiled at the familiar reference. "Proverbs. That's true. I just—I've always loved art. I want to be an artist."

"You *are* an artist—an incredible one. You drew an empty bench, and it made me feel things. That's real talent."

I shrugged one shoulder sadly. "Sure, painting alone in my apartment, with no one to ever see it." I sighed. "I want more, though. I want to sell art, make a living. I want my own shop, with a little gallery, and art supplies, and a place for other people who love it to gather." I looked out over at the horizon, at the sun beginning to melt in a spectacular array of pinks and purples beyond the trees. "Wow."

"It's beautiful," he agreed. "Exactly like you. And if that's really what you want, you should go after it. There's nothing to say you can't have that: your own shop, the gallery—the whole nine yards. It's a great idea." My eyes snapped over to his, drinking in the sincerity I found there.

"You really think so?"

"I do," he said firmly, and reached up to cup my chin in his hand. The gentle caress of his thumb was a happy distraction.

"There's an opportunity at work, actually, that might help. But I don't think I'm even going to make it in the running at this point."

"Why not?"

With a sigh, I pulled away, and his hand fell back to the blanket between us. "I've got nothing. It's a pitch competition, and All I've got is some generic text. No inspiration."

"Hmm, is artist's block a thing?"

"Maybe, I don't know. My painting is coming along well, but this candy company pitch? I've got nothing. It's like, who has something to say about *candy*? And it's this big up and coming company, weirdly. I don't know. The boss has offered a five-thousand-dollar bonus to anyone who can win their business with their pitch. But, at this point I don't have a pitch." I threw my hands up in exasperation. "If I'm being honest, I almost canceled tonight to stay at the office and try to figure something out, but I was sitting there staring at an empty white screen."

"Well, I'm certainly glad you didn't cancel. Besides, isn't all this more inspiring than staring at a computer monitor?" He gestured to the sky, where a beautiful pink and golden show was happening right before our eyes.

"Yes it is, of course. And don't get me wrong, I'm glad I came. Sitting there miserable wouldn't have changed a thing. It's just . . . that money could jump start my big dream, you know?"

"Yeah, absolutely. Well, let's talk about it. Tell me about the company. Let's brainstorm." He picked up a meatball slider and took a big bite, not the least bit bothered by my bringing up work on our date.

"Are you sure? Graphic design isn't super scintillating to most people."

He laughed, and quickly covered his mouth to stop a piece of meatball flying out. "I'm a developer. Software engineering is the one job that everybody wants, but weirdly no one wants to talk about. Unless you're *also* a developer."

"Well, that's because nobody knows the languages. I took a coding class in college, actually. It was interesting, but didn't pull me in the way art always has."

"Oh yeah? That's pretty cool. So, *you* speak my language." He winked and finished off his slider.

"A little bit. I couldn't actually code anything." I took a juicy bite of strawberry, savoring the sweet melt of chocolate on my tongue.

Washing his slider down with some lemonade, he asked again, "That's okay. So, tell me about your client. Let's figure this out together."

"Well, that's the thing. I don't know much about them. The name, candy, a generic list of possible taglines. Really basic, and not a quarter of what we'd usually get."

"Did they give you a product list? Maybe you can find one of their top products, and base it off that? Show that you're paying attention to their business, not only giving them a pretty logo."

"That's . . . a really good idea. Unfortunately, they didn't provide a list. I wonder if it's online somewhere?"

He waved his smartphone at me obligingly. "Let's find out."

In minutes, he'd pulled up an early press release, announcing the expansion from the home store into a nationwide rollout. "Look, the flagship store has photos of the shop, and I can see some menu boards."

He zoomed in, and showed me an antique display case, piled high with handmade candies, and a sign board behind it. The woman behind the counter was smiling, wearing an orange-striped apron. I leaned back on my elbows, staring at the sunset and thinking as he read off a list of products.

"They sell chocolates, mints, hard candies, cotton candy, custom flavored everything for weddings or bar mitzvahs—the works. They even custom make those little gross flavored almonds they served at my cousin's wedding last year. They are like two steps from being Willy Wonka." He grinned and leaned back on his elbows next to me. "You look like you're thinking already. Have you got an idea?"

"I think . . . yes. I think I do. Most candy stores are all hot pink and sprinkles. I didn't want to do the same old, same old, but . . . that apron, and the antique setup. It's unique." I felt something niggling at the back of my mind, like I was on the verge of an ah-ha moment, but I couldn't quite pin it down.

"Yeah, it looks like a cool joint. I hope they open one here."

"Yeah, me too."

We sat in companionable silence for a few moments, and the idea struck. "Sunset colors. Cotton candy, on one of those old-timey paper cone stick things—what are those called?"

He shrugged. "No idea, but I like where you're heading."

"Gosh, why didn't I bring paper? I could sketch it out," I said, mentally berating myself for being unprepared. Though, to be fair, I hadn't expected inspiration to strike on our date, and my sketchbook wouldn't fit in the purse that matched my sundress.

"Hang on, I've got a notepad in the truck." He hopped up, and jogged across to the truck, returning with a white legal pad, and a handful of pens.

"It's nothing like your art supplies, but there's a few different colors, at least," he said as he offered me the lot.

"This is great, thank you!" I immediately flipped to a blank back of a page and began sketching the wispy outline of a cotton candy swirl.

He settled back down next to me, and whispered, "Am I breaking the nobody-sees-it-until-it's-done rule right now? Should I sit over there?"

I stopped drawing and looked over at him, his glasses slightly askew from the jog to fetch the notepad and shook my head. "Nope, stay right where you are. You can tell me what you think. Just this once."

"Just this once," he agreed, and settled in quietly at my side as a cotton candy logo appeared on the page, delicate wisps and swirls nestled atop a paper cone. When I was done, I frowned down at the paper, leaning into the warmth of his arm behind my back.

"I feel like it needs something."

"Well, you said sunset colors, right? So that will make it pop more."

"Yeah, but . . . that's not all. It could be anyone's cotton candy right now. It needs to immediately convey that it's theirs."

He tilted his head, leaning it briefly on my shoulder to get a better view. "What if you add their orange stripes on the cone?" He reached up with his finger and drew where they'd go perfectly along with the slim cone.

"You're pretty smart, you know that?" He shook his head on my shoulder, watching silently as I quickly added in the stripes, imagining them in a bold orange, on a vintage sepia background. Afterward, I hand-lettered the company name winding up and around the treat, and I set the pen down.

"This is beautiful. The fact that you can sit down and do that is impressive. Once you get the colors in, I bet it's going to blow their minds."

"It might, but it's going to be a long weekend. I've got to perfect this, and design a whole branding package, or as much as I can get done, at least."

"Thank you for everything. I'm sorry I took over our date with work. I am probably the worst first date you've ever taken out, huh?" I tucked a strand of hair behind my ear and grimaced apologetically at him.

He shook his head slowly. "Not at all. We talked, we enjoyed tasty food, and I got to watch you work your magic right in front of me. It was actually the *best* first date I've ever been on."

"You're kind of too perfect, you know that?"

"Hardly." He shook his head again, and then leaned over and planted a kiss on my forehead. It was both as natural as breathing and electrifying in the same heartbeat. My breath hitched at the contact, and we froze, an inch apart.

"Sorry, I should have asked, shouldn't I? I shouldn't have kissed you without getting permission. I didn't mean to offend you, I—"

I wrapped my hands around the back of his neck and drew his lips right to mine. The words cut off, and after a moment his shoulders relaxed under my fingertips. Our lips melded together in a sweet tangle, and when I drew back, he had a dazed expression.

"My forehead isn't offended in the slightest," I promised, reaching up to adjust his glasses, where they'd gone askew once again. "My lips might have been, though, if you hadn't kissed them, too."

He grinned, this time slowly, and the sight of his lips curling up at the edges sent heat ricocheting through me like a pinball. He leaned in again, stopping a scant centimeter from my lips. "I definitely don't want to offend these lips. I'd better kiss them one more time, to be sure."

I met him halfway as he pressed forward again, capturing my lips with his in a sweetly torturous kiss. When he pulled back, he twined his fingers with mine, and lifted up our hands to press soft kisses along each knuckle. "I never thought I'd be lucky enough to be the one you wanted to kiss."

SEVEN

The Working Weekend

SIENNA

T he next day at work passed in a frenzy, and yet at the end of the day, I still had too much left to do to take the weekend off if I wanted to submit a fully formed pitch on Monday. So, on Saturday I hauled myself into the office and was unsurprised to see a few other faces also diligently working on their pitches. Around noon, my phone buzzed. I rubbed my tired eyes and grabbed my phone to see who it was.

Finn: I believe day two means sufficient time has passed that I can text and say I'm thinking about you, without coming off as a super-clinger, right? Because I am thinking about you, and I haven't stopped since Thursday night.

Sienna: That's true, the dating rulebook does specify more than twenty-four hours. However, if you go more than forty-eight, it means you don't want a follow-up. You're spot on. *wink emoji*

Finn: Good to know. Could I use my spot-on timing to persuade you to come over and watch a movie with me tonight? Also, a question: is this a literal handbook, or . . . ?

Sienna: I would love that, but to be honest, I'm exhausted. I worked late last night, and I'm back in the office today trying to get this pitch done. I don't know when I'll be done, unfortunately. Also: it's an imaginary handbook. Top secret and all that.

Finn: Totally respect that. I could come to you, or we could do it another time, after the pitch. Your call. I'm down for anything that gets me more Sienna time. Also: someone could make a killing off a literal handbook. I'd buy it.

Finn: It was really great, spending time together.

Finn: And, you know, the kissing was phenomenal, if I may so myself.

The little bubbles popped up one after the other before I'd had a chance to respond, in my tired state. His excitement made me excited, too. Men I'd dated in the past had been aloof, never wanting to give away their thoughts or feelings early on in a relationship. Finn was nothing like anyone I'd ever dated before.

Sienna: It was definitely phenomenal. And I want to spend more time together too, but I'm not sure when I'll have enough energy to get all dolled up. Maybe Tuesday or Wednesday?

Finn: Sienna, I promise I don't care if you get dolled up. You can wear your oldest pair of sweats, and I'll still show up with your favorite pizza order, and a movie. We can veg on the couch.

I wavered; it sounded so tempting, curling up on the couch, watching a movie with my head on his shoulder. But could I really let go and relax? Not do my hair and makeup and put on a nice outfit? Wasn't it too early on for that kind of thing?

Finn: Don't decide now. Finish your work, and text me later. Y or N and I'll take it from there.

Sienna: Deal.

I'd finished the final polish of the logo—including the hand-lettered business name and the digital painting of the cotton candy I'd sketched—plus a sample business card, and a full-page letterhead. When I stopped to rub my gritty eyes, the clock read seven p.m. and I was wiped out. I closed out my computer, stuck my feet back into my long-abandoned shoes, and headed for the parking lot. Before I pulled out of the space, I realized I needed to tell Finn something.

Sienna: Leaving work now. I'm beat. Not sure if we should still do a movie or not. I am dying for a shower.

Finn: Want to take an hour to get home and relax, and I'll bring by pizza and a movie? I won't even complain if you fall asleep ten minutes in. *smile emoji*

I tapped my phone on my chin a few times, debating. I was exhausted, it was true. But, I did have to eat dinner, regardless. The question was, did I want to see Finn again?

I was under no obligation, and neither was he. But, yeah, company would be nice. Someone to come home to—besides an empty apartment—might be nice after two long, hard days of work.

~~*Sienna: It's a date.*~~

~~*Sienna: It's a deal.*~~

Sienna: Sounds like a plan

Finn: I'll saddle my white horse.

I snorted at the corny joke, then drove myself home.

By the time I'd showered and changed, a seed of excitement was starting to bloom. I was still tired, but the idea of spending time with Finn again had me zooming around the living room, artfully arranging my throw blankets "just so" over the arms of the couch. I even dusted, but not until after I'd turned the easel flat against the back wall so there was no chance of accidental viewing.

Satisfied, I pulled some popcorn out of the cabinet right as a knock sounded at the front door.

"Coming!" I abandoned the popcorn and found Finn standing at the front door wearing a video game t-shirt and a wide grin.

"Sienna, hi. I hope you like pepperoni, but I also brought cheese and a veggie lover's. Also, what are your feelings on pineapple on pizza? Some people love it, some people hate it." He asked as he stepped inside, juggling three pizza boxes, a movie case, and a two-liter of soda.

I took the movie and the Coke from him and led him into the kitchen. "Uhm, I'm pretty non-picky where pizza is concerned, and I'm pro-pineapple, but only on Hawaiian, with extra bacon."

"Duly noted for next time." He beamed as he spread out the pizza boxes on the counter. "How did your work turn out? Did you get the designs done for your pitch?"

"It looks amazing, but I didn't get as many options finished as I hoped. If I have time Monday morning, I'll probably try to squeeze in a simple web page layout. A lot of times, the design is great, but you need to make them *see* it by showing the end result."

"That sounds like a lot of work. If they want tweaks, do you have to go back and redo everything?" He looked concerned.

"Basically. Sometimes it's simple, and other times it's a big ol' headache. But, I've had enough work today. I'm ready for some *us* time," I said, doing my best to push aside the weight of possibility lingering over my job right now and focus on the wonderful man in front of me.

"Well then, let's get started on that relaxation we talked about."

"Thank you, my pizza-wielding knight in faded denim. What movie did you pick?" I asked as I flipped the case over. "Jurassic Park?" I raised one eyebrow skeptically as I looked over at him.

"Oh, don't give me that look. It's a classic. Don't tell me you don't want to go for *a walk in the park*." He raised his hands in a ridiculous impersonation of a T-rex, and I laughed, dropping the movie on the counter.

"I can always go for a little nostalgia."

He stepped forward, and dropped his voice to a conspiratorial whisper as he opened his arms, "Could you also go for a hug?"

"Absolutely," I whispered back, and he enveloped me in the best hug I'd had in a long time. I breathed in the scent of his shirt, fresh and clean with a hint of masculinity, and I didn't want to let go. I hugged him back hard, and he gently rubbed my back for a few quiet moments.

I pulled back. "Question, though; why not one of the new ones?"

"Huh? Oh, well, the new ones are *too good*. The graphics are realistic, the acting is stellar . . . Half the fun of JP was being *half*-scared. You know?"

"Well, that is some interesting logic, I'll give you that." I couldn't do anything but shake my head at how his brain worked.

"I was right, you know," he murmured as I dug plates out of the cabinet. "You're every bit as beautiful in a t-shirt with your hair in a bun as you were in your dress."

I turned and passed him a plate, and when I looked up there was nothing but sincerity in his face. "You're pretty handsome yourself, you know."

He ducked his head, shaking it softly, but didn't respond. I got the sense that he didn't have a lot of confidence in that area. A problem to tackle another time, perhaps.

"Is it time for pizza and dinosaurs?" I asked, changing the subject.

He looked up and nodded, a slow smile spreading across his face. "Eight-year-old me would have been *very* impressed that I found a girl who liked this plan."

Then, we both loaded up plates with obscene amounts of pizza, grabbed drinks, and headed for the couch. We settled in, next to each other but not too close, and I got the movie rolling as he turned off all the lights except the lamp. I had barely finished my second slice of pizza, watching the characters ride along in a khaki-colored jeep when a wave of exhaustion washed over me. I shuffled the plate back onto the coffee table and grabbed one of the throw blankets to cover my feet.

"Cold?" he asked, and I shook my head as he settled his arm across the back of the couch.

"Just my feet. My feet always get cold when I'm tired. That's probably weird, huh?" I added belatedly.

"Nah, it's your body's way of tricking you into finding a blanket."

"Probably. I never thought of it that way." Within a few minutes, the screen grew blurry, and I rested my head back against the back of the seat, regretting that I really was going to fall asleep on him so quickly, when he'd gone to all the trouble to come over and feed me dinner.

Without a word, his arm lowered from the back of the couch, encircling my shoulders on the couch. "Hey, I meant it earlier. It's okay if you're tired. You've been under a lot of pressure. If you'll be more comfortable, I will leave now, and you can head to bed."

"No, I don't want you to leave!" I surprised myself by clinging onto his forearm where it rested on my shoulder. "Would it be okay if we just . . . cuddled on the couch? If I start snoring you can wake me up."

"Of course, come on over." He gestured to the small space remaining between me and his side, and I scooched over to close the distance.

Within moments, his comforting smell and the warmth from his side had lulled me into peaceful slumber.

As my eyes slid shut, I thought I heard him whisper, "Sweet dreams, my angel."

Finn

As Sienna's eyes slid shut, I dropped a kiss on top of her head, and settled in to finish the movie. It might have been cheesy, but it was my favorite, and I'd wanted to share it with her. After the movie ended I'd get her comfortable on the couch, put the pizza in the fridge, and lock up on my way out. Though, my mind was moving a thousand miles an hour, and it wasn't on nineties graphics.

She'd said yes. This wasn't a town setup; it was completely obligation-free. And yet, here we were.

I was pretty sure in the beginning that she'd only bid on me out of a sense of lingering friendship, to save me from humiliation. And I appreciated that, truly, even if it was mortifying. *Thanks, Aunt Dolly.*

When you live in a small town like we do, the dating pool is small. Once most of the women have decided you're not the one, well . . . there's online dating, and then there's other locations. There's no third option—not really—and for some reason I'd never been anyone's idea of Prince Charming.

I didn't play sports in high school; I went to coding camps. While everyone else was sneaking off to the overlook, I was at home, filling out college scholarship applications so I could afford to go to school. It worked out for me, and now I'm happy with who I am, but I'm not Mr. Popular, not like George. He's so good with people, unlike me. If it weren't for Sienna, I'd have absolutely been up the auction-block creek.

But then, she'd kissed me. Full on grabbed me by the back of the neck and planted one on me that shook me to my roots. And suddenly, middle school friendship was the last thing on my mind. She was all grown up, and I didn't want anything so much as to see her again. And again, and again. She'd intrigued me since my earliest memories of her, always straight as an arrow.

Whatever she wanted, she went for it with no hesitation. Brave, sure of herself, and dead-on-target.

And she said yes. Smart as a whip, unfailingly kind, and the most gorgeous woman I'd ever laid eyes on; she was more than I could ever deserve. I looked down at her face, relaxed in sleep, and couldn't think of anywhere else in the world I'd rather be. She shifted, mumbling something in her sleep and tucking her cheek further into my shoulder, making her blanket slip down. I pulled it back up over her shoulder, careful not to disturb her with the motion.

It was actually surprising to hear she had a dream she hadn't gone straight for, but I had already decided to help her with that, if she'd let me. I knew the guy who owned the shop; I'd made his website a few years ago. If she won her pitch bonus, I could get him to give her the first three month's rent and an abatement period for less than that. Even if she didn't win the contest—hard to imagine, even her basic sketches were brilliant—I knew we could figure it out.

And I could make her a website for the shop. I didn't know anything about art that wasn't a series of CSS codes, but I could learn. For her, I'd learn. I watched blindly as raptors hunted through the park, already mentally planning out a web store for her new art shop.

Eight

T-r-o-u-b-l-e

Sienna

I woke with a groan, my neck stiff as day-old modeling clay. Blinking a few times, it took me a moment to realize why I wasn't in my bed. Oh, I fell asleep on the couch last night, right next to—Finn. I froze, realizing my cheek was pressed against a warm, firm chest, his t-shirt rumbled under my fingertips.

Sometime during the night, he'd fallen asleep too, and we'd shifted against the arm of the couch. He was still breathing deeply, sound asleep, and I took the opportunity to study his profile from my position smooshed against his side. He had a straight nose with a slight bump, leading me to his wide, perfectly bowed lips. Heat infused my cheeks as I remembered kissing him, and I quickly looked up, where dark lashes lay on his cheeks, hiding his gorgeous hazelnut eyes. His hair was dark and thick, and I gave into the temptation to push a few strands away from his face, reveling in the softness between my fingers.

He stirred and I froze again, debating how best to extricate myself without waking him up. I started to roll backward, slowly putting space between us, when the couch abruptly ran out of real estate, and I found myself flat on my back next to the coffee table, staring up at the ceiling. I wheezed quietly, trying to get off my back about as successfully as a turtle stuck on its shell.

Finally—engaging those oft-overlooked abs—I surged upright and tiptoed out of the room. I needed coffee, stat, and to figure out how to sneak Finn out of here before my neighbor realized he'd stayed the whole night. On the couch or no, tongues would be wagging by the end of the hour if my neighbor Jolene spotted him.

A quick perusal confirmed that the fridge was sadly devoid of food, so, hopefully he didn't mind getting breakfast elsewhere. With work taking all my focus, I hadn't shopped yet for the week. At least there was plenty of coffee.

A couple minutes later, I was filling two mugs with the sweet, sweet nectar that is dark roast when Finn cleared his throat behind me.

"I'm sorry I fell asleep on your couch," he said with a grimace. "I had every intention of leaving when the movie was over, but I don't think I lasted long after you fell asleep."

"Oh, it's okay. No big deal. I'm pretty sure my ear left an indent on your arm. Coffee?" I held out the second cup, and he accepted it.

"Thanks, sugar?"

"Why yes, I am sweet." I passed him the sugar dish with a wink.

He chortled and scooped three heaping spoonfuls into the mug. "Yes you are, no arguments there. Hey, I was thinking about it last night—have you got any ideas for your art shop's name?"

Stunned that that's what he was thinking about, I waffled about for an answer. "Well, no. It doesn't exist yet, and until this week I was pretty sure it would never exist, outside my dreams. So, no. I might be one of those gauche people who names it after myself. Or maybe I'll think of something creative. Or artsy? Probably would be good if the shop name indicated that it sold art supplies, and art."

"Mm, like that mysterious painting I'm dying to see?" he asked, taking a long pull of his coffee.

"Yes, that kind."

He grinned, and I grinned right back on reflex. We finished our coffees in comfortable silence, and then he rinsed it out in the sink. "I should probably get out of your hair. I know you've been working hard all week, and you didn't expect an overnight guest."

Was that a blush I spied creeping up to his earlobes?

"No, but that's okay. I also didn't expect pizza delivery, a movie night, and amazing company, but those were all good things. *Really* good things." I reached out and captured his hand, twining his fingers in mine.

"Good, I'm glad. I'll call you soon, maybe set up a real date—the kind where we go out and I buy you dinner at a fancy place?" he asked, taking a step closer.

"I don't need fancy, but I do always love Jude's." I set my coffee cup down on the counter, not bothering to rinse it since I knew I'd have another.

"It's a date, then. Jude's for dinner, and then we can stop by the bakery after to celebrate your win on the pitch." He leaned closer, and I shifted from one foot to the other, anticipating a kiss.

It was a simple kiss, only a few seconds of contact, but still sent excitement down to the tips of my toes. I could get used to that. The thought was both exciting and terrifying. What if I got used to him being around, us being together—used to having someone who meant so much to me—and then he left?

I shoved the negative thought aside and walked him to the front door. It wasn't fair to put my issues with my dad on him; he'd been nothing but amazing so far. Not to mention, it was still so, so early. *Two dates, and I was worried about him running off? What I should be worried about was getting him past Mrs. Jolene next door*, I chastised myself firmly. I peeked out the front window and didn't see her outside. Taking a deep breath, I quickly opened it to let him out.

He stepped out on the front porch and turned, speaking quickly, "I'll call you Monday, or you call me first if you get good news. Or bad news. But I have no doubts you're going to win this thing. Either way, we'll do dinner, okay?"

"Okay, thank you, Finn. For the pizza, and the support, and for always . . . believing in me." I shrugged one shoulder, feeling silly for laying it all out there. "That might sound dumb. But it means a lot that you're so confident." I dropped my eyes to a worn front-porch plank.

He stepped forward, closing the distance between us, and lifted my chin with a fingertip. "That's better. Never feel silly with me, Sienna. You have big dreams, and I love that about you. Of course I'm confident. Remember that time in Mr. Baum's class when it was time to do the frog dissections?"

"Uhm, yes? It was gross, I remember that."

"Yeah, it was gross. But I remember that I felt queasy at the thought, and you were absolutely fearless. Everyone else in the whole class was complaining, but not you. You aced it, like everything else they put in front of you. Even then, nothing slowed you down."

I snorted at the memory. "Just because I don't show it doesn't mean I don't feel afraid, Finn. Everyone feels afraid."

"Of course, they do. But you? You never let it stop you. And I have complete faith that you'll make your dream art shop a reality." He leaned forward and was about to kiss me again when Mrs. Jolene from next door called out, and we jolted apart in surprise.

"Well! Look at that, a pair of love birds. And so early on the Lord's Day! My, how lucky you are to have such a dedicated suitor," she cooed, lifting a single eyebrow as she loudly sipped her coffee. "My Merle was devoted from the start."

"Good morning, Mrs. Jolene. How are you today?" Finn called out, perfectly polite, even as I was dying inside. She must have been sitting in the chair at the very back corner of her porch; she'd probably seen him come out.

"Wonderful, darling. Will we see you at church this morning? I'm sure Dolly will have a seat for you."

"Yes ma'am, I'll be heading there shortly."

"Good, I'll see you there. Now, I've got to go get my curlers out. You two behave, now." She gave me a pointed look, and then turned and walked inside, ample hips swaying.

"So, how fast do you think she's going to call my Aunt Dolly?" he asked wryly.

"Probably already is," I said through gritted teeth.

"Ahh, small towns," he said, then leaned forward, bracketing me against the door with his hands and whispered, "If we already got caught, I think we may as well get that kiss, right?"

I waffled for a split second, then nodded. He planted a teasing kiss on my lips, gave my fingers a squeeze, and then pulled back, casting a glance at my neighbor's porch. "I'd better go before she calls in reinforcements to come and gawk. We'll talk soon."

"You don't have to wait a whole day this time," I teased, eliciting a shy chuckle from Finn as he walked away. I shut the door and stood in the window, watching until his truck pulled out of sight.

With a sigh, I wandered to the bathroom to get ready for the day, and headed out to get groceries.

As I climbed out of the car at the grocery store, I made my grumbling stomach a promise: if I made it through the shopping trip without buying every type of junk food in sight, I'd stop by the bakery on the way home. Sweet Nothings had these little pastries with a cherry center that were my all-time favorite weekend brunch. Grocery shopping on an empty stomach? Definitely earned it.

Reusable bags in tow, I nodded at Lena who was manning the customer service counter and got down to business. I had half-filled my cart with all the good stuff and was turning onto the cookie-and-cracker aisle for some crackers to go with my chicken salad lunches when I overheard two women talking and froze in my tracks.

"Mm-hmm. Matched last week at the auction, and already having a sleepover! I tell you, Dolly's head's going to explode when she hears. Frankly, if it wasn't Sunday, I wager she'd already be taking her scoundrel of a nephew to task for his behavior."

Color flooded my cheeks, and I prayed the ground would open up and swallow me as the other woman responded. No such luck—I guess that's what I got for grocery shopping instead of hitting my usual pew on Sunday.

"It's shocking, really. The matron's league were hoping a few weddings might result from introducing the town singles, but I don't think they were planning for them to be *shotgun weddings*." The first woman tittered, and their voices grew distant as they proceeded down the aisle.

Suddenly, I lost my appetite for crackers and chicken salad. Even the good stuff with the grapes in it. Backing up my cart, I made a beeline for the checkout—but not before I stopped and checked that the lane was empty of gossips.

I had a sinking feeling it was far from the last I'd be hearing about my impending shotgun wedding.

I took a deep breath to steel myself, and then pulled open the door to the Sweet Nothings Bake Shop. It was a quaint little place, the friendly pink gingham and cafe-style tables inviting you to sit a while and linger over the fine baked goods displayed in the cases. It didn't hurt that Celia, the owner, was the nicest lady in town, and no matter what she heard, she wouldn't judge me for it. It was a safe zone, and a retreat I desperately needed.

The seats were completely empty, while the bakery displays were blessedly full. I spotted an entire tray of my favorite cherry pastries and made a bee-line for the counter.

Celia wandered out from the back, flour-dusted apron on and a towel tossed over her shoulder. "Good morning, Sienna. No church today?"

"No, ma'am. It was a rough week at work, and I had to catch up on some things around the house . . . I'll be back next week, though." *Assuming I could show my face.*

"I'm sure you will, honey. Don't worry, God will meet you wherever you call him. What can I get for you this morning?"

"Hmm, I need a cherry pastry, as usual. What special do you recommend?"

Without hesitation, she plated up the pastry, and grabbed an intricately shaped donut from a second case. Balancing it all with ease, she spun to grab a coffee cup. "The usual coffee?"

"Yes, thank you."

She worked in efficient silence, passing me the plate, and retreating with the cup to fill it. I stood stock still and watched, my brain in knots about how the morning had gone from contentment with Finn to trouble with the whole town in the course of an hour.

When she spun around and set the coffee on the counter, she paused, taking in my unusual silence.

"Honey, what's going on?"

"Ahh, well . . . there's a pretty embarrassing rumor floating around town. About me. And a man . . . Finn. The man is Finn," I rambled, and she leaned her hip against the counter to wait me out.

"I do seem to remember you two getting matched up at the auction. Is that what's caused it?"

I shook my head and looked down at the scuffed and paint-splattered toes of my favorite Chucks. I really needed to clean them one of these days. "No. Well, not directly. Nobody cares about the auction, since it was all public and a lot of people were matched. He came over to watch a movie last night, and Mrs. Jolene saw him leaving . . . this morning."

"Ahh," she said, drawing out the short word across several syllables. "And this didn't go over well?"

"No. Everyone's making assumptions. Embarrassing assumptions, when the truth is that we watched an old movie and fell asleep—fully clothed—on the couch. And I mean, we're both grown adults. Surely the town has something better to talk about, even if what they suspected *were* true." I surprised myself with the angry outburst, and clamped my lips shut to stop more from pouring out on Celia, who most likely had something waiting on her back in the kitchen.

But she didn't go back to the kitchen, and she didn't question or accuse me. Instead, she reached across the counter, and placed her hand on mine, where I'd balled them up into fists on the counter without realizing it.

"Honey, it's going to be all right. Do you want to know a secret?"

"What's that?"

"Everybody gets afoul of the town rumor mill every once in a while. It's a hazard of small-town living. I understand feeling embarrassed, having a relationship coming under scrutiny. Especially such a new one. But don't let that get to you. It's like you said; you're a grown woman, and you can stay up every night watching movies with anyone you please. As long as you know deep down that you didn't do a thing wrong, it doesn't matter one iota what any of these bored townsfolk say. Besides, they'll be chasing the other couples too, looking for the next scoop." She smiled and squeezed my hand.

"I know, and you're right. It's just so embarrassing. I was in the grocery store an hour later and people were already talking about us. I was mortified. I should probably buy the whole row of pastries, so I can drown my sorrows in cherry filling," I grumbled.

Celia laughed and smacked the towel down on the countertop. "Well, it would be good for business, but I don't think you need to, Sienna. You and Finn are good people; everybody knows it, and nobody wants to see you fail—if you're pursuing a relationship, that is. Give it a day, maybe two, and some of the teenage boys in this town will rustle up an alligator or try to walk a raccoon on a leash. Something crazy, guaranteed, and the talk will blow right over."

"I hope so. I really, really hope so. Dating is hard enough, but add humiliation on top . . ." I swallowed hard and reached for the coffee to have something to do with my mouth besides talk. I took a quick swallow, then asked, "How much do I owe you? I'm willing to pay extra for the wise advice."

"On the house, and I'll box you up an extra pastry to go, too. You've earned it."

"Celia, you should let me pay."

"Ah-ah—don't pull out that wallet or I'll be offended. Go enjoy your treats and I'll bring you the box. *And* if anyone comes in here spreading gossip, I'll remind them about some of the embarrassing things they've done over the years, and how tragic it would be if word of those went 'round again." She winked, and relief washed over me. Embarrassingly, tears of gratitude pricked the corners of my eyes, and I hurried to a table at the back corner where she wouldn't see them.

I said a quick prayer of thanks, and then made a point to pull out my e-reader and put aside my worry about the gossip. Celia was right; people might talk, but it *would* blow over. I was a grown woman, and I had nothing to be ashamed of.

Finn

I made it to the third row of pews before I heard the first giggle. The fourth row, and it felt like eyes were burning tracks into my back. By the time I reached row eight where my aunt and uncle always sat, I'm pretty sure I saw someone pointing out of the corner of my eye. Keeping my eyes forward, I slid onto the stiff wooden pew, and slid across to sit next to my Uncle Steve.

"Morning, Uncle Steve, Aunt Dolly." I nodded and leaned back against the seat. My back had barely touched wood when I heard a smack on his arm.

"Move over, Steve. Me and Finny need to have a talk."

My uncle, ever a man of few words, grunted and stood, allowing my Aunt Dolly to slide into his space. He sat down on her other side, and continued reading the bulletin, soundly ignoring the tempest heading straight my way.

"Everything okay, Aunt Dolly?"

"Finnegan Jack Russell, don't you act coy with me. Jolene called me in the wee hours this morning, and told me"—she glanced quickly around, then lowered her voice to a theater whisper—"that your *truck* was still outside that girl Sienna's house. Then, she called again, crowing about how you left in the same clothes she saw you bringing pizza in last night! Now, I do not want to have my ears sullied with any sordid details—in the house of the Lord, no less—but Finnegan, you had better tell me right now what you think you were doing! Our family has standards. We have *morals*. And you, sir, did *not* uphold them last night." She was so angry, that even when she stopped dressing me down, her chin continued to wobble for several seconds.

"Aunt Dolly, I promise you that absolutely nothing against our family's morals happened, and furthermore—"

"But the *appearance* of impropriety is no better, Finn! You are such a good boy; I hate that you've been brought down by association with that woman already. She's so bohemian, and what's a good boy like you to do—"

"Now wait a dadgum minute, Aunt Dolly. Sienna didn't do anything wrong, either. In fact, I was the one who pursued *her*, asked her to have me over. Not the other way around. And once again, I repeat, nothing at all happened, besides two grown adults watching a nineties classic movie, and falling asleep. *That is all.* And I am not going to sit here and listen to you—or anybody else in this town—imply otherwise."

"Finn, lower your voice!" she hissed, glancing warily at the dozens of eyes no doubt pinned on us.

"I don't think I'm in the mood for church today, Uncle Steve. I'm going home."

"Don't blame you. Have a good one," he said blandly, never even glancing up from his bulletin, despite the steam practically billowing out of his wife's ears.

"Finnegan! Sit back down this instant. This is going to do nothing but add fuel to the fire, and we do not want that." She gave me her best threatening glare—the one that always made me hop-to and straighten up as a kid, even when I hadn't done a blasted thing wrong—but it rolled right off. Today, I had righteous indignation on my side.

I turned out of the pew and stared down anybody who dared to gawk as I left the sanctuary. The assistant pastor patted me on the back as I passed him in the aisle on my way out.

"See you next week, Finn."

"See you then, Brother Lee."

NINE

Wrenches . . .

SIENNA

Monday morning rolled around, and I was actually grateful to go into work. Nobody there would know or care about the town drama since it was forty-five minutes' drive out of town. Tamika caught me as I charged in the door like a bull with my head down, pulling me into her cubicle.

"Girl, you look like somebody stole the last sip of coffee straight out of your cup. What's wrong? Is it the presentation? Everybody knows you're the best, even if they don't pick yours—you know that, right? There's no accounting for taste these days." She gave me a sympathetic look, and my stomach turned over miserably.

"No, Tamika. I mean, yes, I've still got work to do before noon. I could really use that money, so I'd love to win. But . . . the weekend took a turn. Personal drama."

Her eyes widened, and she leaned in, her face a picture of morbid curiosity as she clutched the edge of the desk for balance. "Not the geek chic hottie, right? Please tell me he's not a jerk. I have plans for him if you two don't work out."

I paused, momentarily taken aback. Even after three years working together, Tamika still surprised me all the time. "You're nuts, but I love you. And no, not him. I mean, it was because of him, but he didn't do anything wrong. But . . . the town gossips got ahold of us, and it was bad."

"Does that mean something juicy happened?" She waggled her eyebrows. "You know I'm all for juicy."

"I know, but no. I mean, yes. Ahh, I don't know anymore, Tamika." I raked my fingers through my hair, not caring if I messed it up. I hadn't even styled it, only clipped it back and forgot about it. "We kissed."

"Ooh . . . yes! Tell me about it! Was it good? Was he good? Wait, back up. Where were you, what was the setup, and—"

"Tamika, the presentations are due in . . . less than three and a half hours. We do not have time for this.

Not to mention, I don't want to give Bryan's fan club the same gossip I'm trying to escape."

She narrowed her eyes and stood up, gazing around the office for any of his cronies. "You let me worry about them. They say anything to you, and I'll wipe the floor with their sorry rear ends."

She meant every word, and I loved her for it. "How about we have a girls' lunch, and catch up after we submit? I will tell you about my roller coaster weekend once all this is behind us."

"Deal. Go work, you good employee, you. I'll just be over here imagining your first kiss with the handsome geek."

"His name's Finn."

"Shh, that's not important. His cheekbones tell me all I need to know." She waved me away as she settled back into her chair and flipped on her monitor, to put the final touches on her own pitch.

While Tamika was a supportive friend and insisted I was the best designer, she was every bit as skilled, and could give me a run for my money any day of the week. If she had time to chat, it was because she was a fast, efficient worker, something Bryan and team should have paid better attention to. Although, Tamika liked to fly under the radar and surprise people, I mused as I slid into my own chair.

I was only five minutes into the web layout when Bryan poked his head over the top wall of my cubicle.

"Good morning, Sienna. How's that project coming?"

"Great, Bryan. How's yours?"

"Excellent. Completely done, ready to present. I was considering walking it up to Randy early, so he'd have some extra time to peruse it."

"Well, have fun with that." I pointedly looked back down at my open project, but he didn't leave.

"He's not in yet, so I thought I'd check on how everyone else was doing. You know, that's the kind of thing the assistant art director does."

I sighed and minimized the project. "Have you been made the assistant art director already?"

"No, but taking the initiative can't hurt." He double-tapped the wall of my cubicle and meandered off to hassle the next designer who was frantically putting the final touches on their project. Actually, it was kind of odd that he wasn't busy doing the same. Either he was overconfident in his superiority, or he really had already put together a completely polished product. I guess we'd find out when the final five projects were chosen.

At eleven fifty-five, I closed out the project, zipped up all of the files, and uploaded them to the special work board specifically for the new client pitch competition. I watched as file after file populated, and heads began to pop up around the office, like prairie dogs coming out of their work holes, once their submissions were complete.

My phone vibrated, and I checked it idly.

Finn: Knock them dead today, Sienna. Your concept is beautiful, and you deserve this. I'd love to take you out to lunch, if you need a distraction.

Tamika rapped on the side of my cubicle as she stopped in the entryway to chat. "Girl, I got it in under the wire. Are you all wrapped up? I could use some food—two hours ago."

"Uhm, maybe?" I quickly tapped out a reply to Finn.

Sienna: All submitted. I thought we were going to have dinner? Unless you can't.

The typing bubble popped up, and I looked back up at Tamika, who wore a cheese-eating grin. "Girl, you have got it bad for Finn. I can't wait to hear about your spicy weekend. Maybe I should move on down to Adele. It seems like I'd make a real splash." She mimed jumping into a pool right as my phone vibrated again, making me laugh.

"Go on and check with lover boy. I'll wait." She grabbed a ChapStick out of her purse, already ready to walk out the door.

Finn: No, I'm still on for dinner. It's just so far away.

Sienna: Unfortunately, so am I. By the time you got here and turned back around, your lunch break would be over, and you'd still be hungry.

Finn: We need to get your shop opened STAT, so I can drop in for casual lunch Mondays.

Sienna: Only Mondays?

Finn: I like the way you think. See you at six thirty?

Sienna: It's a date. XOXO

Finn: I'm not sure which of those is hugs, and which is kisses, but I'll google it. XOXO

"Oh my God, he is cuuuute!" Tamika crowed from her position not-so-stealthily reading over my shoulder. "Does he have a brother? Cousin? Identical twin separated at birth?"

I groaned. "Tamika, don't say the t-word. And yes, let's get lunch."

"Ooh, that means you've got news about MIA Suze, too. This is going to be good." She moonwalked backwards out of my cubicle, and I grabbed my purse and followed her out of the office, a few of our fellow prairie dogs waving at us as we left. Life was never boring with Tamika.

Tamika and I took a long lunch, and I filled her in on all the embarrassing details of the day before. She was irate on my behalf, and this time offered to move to Adele to "kick some prim, no-account, gossip-slinging butt." I assured her that butt-kicking wasn't necessary, even if I did appreciate her unwavering loyalty. She was a good friend.

Bellies full of tacos, we were walking back into the office when a meeting invite for two p.m. came through, to announce the top five campaigns being submitted to the client.

"That was fast. That means the competition was either slim pickings, or so spectacular it was an easy choice. Either way, they aren't wasting time."

"It's better that way. No time to endlessly torture ourselves with the possibilities."

"True, true." We parted ways to head to our desks and waited out the remaining half hour before the meeting.

I'd barely sat down when my phone went off, again. Expecting another note from Finn, I was surprised to see it was the group text with Jenny and Marlie.

J: GIRRRRRL *what is this I hear about Finn storming out of church yesterday after a screaming match with his aunt?*

My jaw dropped, and my palms started to sweat. Finn had gotten into it with Dolly? In front of the whole town . . . *at church?!*

M: *It wasn't a screaming match, Jenny. Don't freak her out. Mom said it was just raised voices. No screaming.*

I closed my eyes for a second, deep-seated embarrassment threatening to overwhelm me. I was a private person. It was bad enough that people were whispering about us. But public displays? That was so far out of my comfort zone I couldn't see it from space. So, so far.

S: *This is the first I'm hearing of it.*

J: *You'd better call your man. He needs to give you the dish.*

M: *What does that even mean? Did getting pregnant suddenly make me ten years behind on slang?*

J: *Dish is like tea.*

M: *. . . ?*

J: *Not the point. The point is, our girl S is in the dark, and she shouldn't be.*

S: *To be fair, I didn't tell him about the run-in at the grocery store yesterday, yet. Maybe never.*

M: *What happened at the grocery store?*

J: *Which grocery store? I heard somebody went into labor at the Publix yesterday.*

M: *That's so not fair. It's my turn to go into labor next.* WHY WON'T THIS BABY COME OUT?

J: *1. Because you married a stubborn giant. 2. Not the point. Still need to know who ran into what/who at the grocery store.*

My five-minute reminder for the meeting dinged, pulling me out of their back and forth.

S: *Can't talk now, heading into a big meeting. We can swap details later.*

I switched the phone to silent and headed into the meeting.

I clearly wasn't the only one anxious for news because despite being a couple minutes early, the room was nearly full. I opted to stand near the door, leaning against the wall of the conference room. Randy's personal secretary Barbara came in next, and fidgeted with the projector display for a moment, and then Tamika walked in with Randy right behind.

He clapped once, a big grin on his face as he strode to the center of the conference room. "All right, everyone! Your submissions were better than I'd hoped on such short notice—once again underlining that we here at Bosch & Harvey design have the best design team out there. So, I want to start by saying thank you to everyone for giving it your all; even if your design wasn't selected, that doesn't mean it wasn't top quality, and I actually have alternate clients in mind for a few of you. Celeste will be reaching out to you tomorrow to set up meetings about those. Now, who's ready to see the top five?"

Tense silence was his only answer. "Okay, okay. Celeste, have you got the pointer? Perfect, thank you." He accepted the remote and turned towards the wall screen.

With the click of a button, the first presentation went up on the board. I had to bite back a groan, because *of course* it was Bryan's. His name was emblazoned above a clean-cut black and white logo, the stylized pile of candies decorated with a range of designs. Randy didn't linger, though, reading off names, giving a pause for everyone to view the logo, and then flipping to the next.

"Bryan, Reese, Tamika, Lou, and Sienna."

I let out a breath as he called my name, flashing my brightly swirling cotton candy logo onto the display. It was a stark contrast to some of the others, but it still felt right to me. Tamika gave me a double thumbs up from her position behind Randy, and I returned a smile.

"Congratulations everyone, and as a thank you for the hard work, you're all free to go home early for the afternoon. We don't expect an answer until Wednesday or Thursday, but I've got a good feeling. Those of you who were chosen, please take the next few days to button up any other projects you have ongoing; this is going to move very quickly once a selection is made, and I want each of you to be available."

I walked out of the conference room with a spring in my step, and all but bolted for the door after a quick goodbye to Tamika. I had an unexpectedly free afternoon, and a date to get ready for.

Finn

I could not catch a break. Not one. The routine server maintenance had gone sideways, resulting in an outage. While it wasn't unheard of, it left me as the project lead holding their hands, even though I wasn't over the server team. *Their* leader was in Hawai'i, the lucky duck, while I was stuck here, not allowed to leave until every single server was back up and running. I checked the clock for the hundredth time, and saw it tick over once again. Five fifty-nine.

I opened up the company messaging app and fired off a quick message to the team working on the outage.

Finn: Team, any ETA on a green light to re-deploy?
Jorge: Probably a couple hours, max.
Tony: Nah, man. I think we're here until midnight. Are you ordering pizza? Yuri always gets us pizza for overnights. I like mine with black olives and mush-rooms.

Jorge: That's why nobody lets you order the pizza, Tony. We want cheese.

With a sigh, I shoved back from the keyboard, wearily laying my head back against my desk chair and closing my eyes. They were gritty, and even closed I could see code playing behind them like a low-budget movie. I took off my glasses, rubbing for a moment to try to get them loosened back up.

Even though I was loath to do it, it was time to stop my wishful thinking, and send Sienna a mes-sage. I wasn't making it to dinner.

Unless you counted olive pizza with Tony, which I did not.

Sliding my glasses back into place, I picked up my cell, and tapped out the last message I wanted to send.

Sienna

Painted toenails? Check.

Shaved legs? Check.

My best black dress? Check.

Hair artfully styled to look like I woke up this way, even though it took forty-five minutes? Double-check.

My phone buzzed on my dresser, and I stepped away from the full-length mirror on the bathroom door to check it. Hopefully Finn would be his usual punctual self, because I was *starving*. It was a lot of work getting ready for a date, and frankly, Finn was the first person I'd felt like putting in the effort for in a long time. He was so sweet, and always supportive of my dreams. Even when I wasn't sure they were going to work, myself.

Finn: Hey Sienna, I absolutely hate to send this message, but unfortunately I have to cancel dinner. One of the teams I'm overseeing has an outage, and we can't leave until it's done. It might be soon, but it might be after midnight. I will make it up to you as soon as humanly possible, but unfortunately I can't get free tonight. I hope you'll understand. XOXO Finn

Well, that sucked. I flopped down on the end of the bed, deflated after my afternoon of pampering and preparation. I jiggled my phone back and forth a few times like a paintbrush, trying to decide what to say.

Sienna: I understand, no worries. I'm sorry you've got to stay late, though. I'll take you up on the offer of a make-up date. Are they at least feeding you sometime between now and midnight?

Finn: You're the best. There has been talk of olive pizza.

Sienna: Don't you hate veggie pizza?

Finn: You remembered.

Sienna: Of course. *kiss emoji*

Finn: You know how to make me feel special. *kiss emoji*

I grinned, imagining the short, sweet messages in his warm, humor-tinged voice. He always had a good attitude, even when a situation was bad. An idea struck me.

Sienna: Stay safe out there. Don't eat any questionable pizza, and call me when you're done with work.

Finn: Deal.

I dropped the phone into my dress pocket, slid on my favorite sparkly flats, and headed out the door.

The line at Gianni's was long, even on a Monday night. However, that's because everybody in Adele knew it was the only place worth mentioning with Italian. I hopped into the line, inching forward towards the hostess's stand to place my order, and drooling over the divine smells of bread, cheese, and Italian herbs wafting through the air like Gianni's ancestors had personally blessed the place. They might have; the food was that good.

I was swaying along to the upbeat music when I caught a woman glaring at me from the front of the line. I didn't recognize her, but she seemed to recognize me, based on the number of ugly looks she sent my way as the line moved forward. After she placed her order, she sent me one last nasty glare, flicked her blonde hair over her shoulder, and sauntered away to the drink station as if it was a statement.

What in the world have I done to tick this woman off? I glanced around nervously, not wanting any more scenes to draw attention, with the town already buzzing around me and Finn. Thankfully, no one else was looking my way, and the woman stayed across the restaurant as I made my way to the front counter. She typed furiously on her phone, but the glaring stopped.

I was next in line when it hit me. Had she mistaken me for Suze? My sister was not above stealing a boyfriend if it suited her—or even the occasional lipstick, much to my chagrin. While we didn't dress the same, it was probable that a passing acquaintance would mistake us. The only question was, what had my sister done to this poor lady; and should I address it, or keep my distance? I cast a quick glance her way, and she was glaring in my direction again as I reached the front.

Distance. *Definitely* distance. Whatever Suze had done, there was no need for me to catch the brunt of it. *I got enough of that at work, thank you very much.*

I ordered a large pizza and garlic knots from Gianni's cousin Giorgia, then quickly shuffled off to the opposite side of the restaurant to wait in an empty seat towards the back. With any luck, the woman would get her food and save her wrath for the real Suze.

It wasn't long before they called my name to pick up, and I breathed a sigh of relief as I backed out the glass front door with my oversized dinner.

When I spun around to walk to my car, the mystery woman was standing there, take-out bag in one hand, and the other propped on her hip. She looked mad enough to spit nails, and I froze, allowing the

door to slip free. I winced as it slammed shut behind m
e.

"So, you think you can go around stealing people's boyfriends, huh? Didn't anyone ever teach you the girl code? If a guy's taken, you should *move on* to greener pastures."

"Uhm, I think you've got the wrong person? I haven't stolen anyone's—"

"Oh, don't try that. I know you've got a twin. It's wrong, is what I'm saying. He's mine, back off. Everyone knows we're getting back together." She took a step forward and I instinctively stepped back, the pizza boxes feeling like a meager shield for the tidal wave of fury she emitted.

"Who is this about, exactly? I can call my sister. I mean, she might not answer—she isn't too happy with me at the moment—but I'm willing to try." I ground to a halt as she rolled her eyes.

"Wow, what does Finn see in you? He usually goes for *smart* girls. You're pretty enough, I suppose, but bless your heart, you can't even figure out that I know you're not Suze." My jaw dropped, horror washing over me. Was this *Finn's* ex-girlfriend? How had I missed that he had a girlfriend serious enough that she thought he was coming back?

"I don't know what to say—"

"Don't say anything." She cut me off. "Just remember, he was mine first, and I *will* get him back. Don't get too comfy, thinking you're all coupled up because of a stupid *charity* event." She spun on her heel, once again flicking her sun-bleached locks over her shoulder, then sauntered away and climbed into a baby blue Prius. The way she said charity made it clear that she thought I was the charity case in Finn's and my budding relationship, and it stung.

The door creaked behind me and jolted me into motion. I hurried back to my car, horrified by what the people inside the restaurant probably thought after that very public showdown. Was this relationship doomed to crash on the town drama iceberg? It suddenly felt an awful lot like I was treading water in the arctic; or maybe that was a result of the ice in my veins at the idea of Finn leaving me to go back to her.

TEN

... with a Side of Pizza

SIENNA

Fifteen minutes later, I stood in front of the over-sized revolving door to Finn's office frozen in indecision. Did I go in? Did I go home and pretend this never happened? I'd wanted to surprise him, but after the run-in with Cindy, I really wanted to hide under a rock.

My phone buzzed in my pocket, breaking my concentration.

Finn: I'm sorry I had to cancel. I was really looking forward to dinner tonight and seeing your beautiful smile.

I couldn't help a small smile at his words. A flutter of excitement bloomed in my stomach, edging out the uncertainty. Finn had been nothing but good and kind to me so far. I could give him a chance to explain what was going on with his ex. I'd want him to give me a chance, if the situation were reversed. Steeling my spine, I snapped a quick photo of me outside his office door and sent it to him with a reply.

Sienna: *Funny you should say that . . . up for a pizza delivery?*

Finn: *I'm coming down! Don't move a muscle!*

I slid my phone back into my pocket, and within two minutes, Finn was rounding the corner inside and waving me through the door. I stepped through, and he immediately took the pizza boxes, sliding them onto the security guard's desk, and wrapped me in a bear hug. He spun us in a circle, pulling out a giggle, and lifting my feet from the floor in the process.

"Finn!"

"Sorry, sorry." He set me back on my feet, and briefly touched my cheek with his fingertip. "I'm just so glad to see you! This is the best surprise. Can you come up and have a slice with me?"

His eyes were hopeful, and the knot of tension between my shoulder blades loosened. "Absolutely."

He nodded to the bemused guard and led me by the hand down the hall and to an elevator. We rode up to the top floor in happy silence, him bouncing on the balls of his feet and balancing pizza boxes, me holding his free hand in both of mine.

The elevator dinged, and he led me out into a small sea of beige cubicles. Abstract art adorned the walls in the least exciting way possible, and within thirty seconds I knew I'd hate to stare at these life-less tan-and-blue prints every day. He wove across the floor, never letting go of my fingers as we approached a bank of glass offices lining a wall of floor-to-ceiling windows. Kicking the door open with his foot, Finn led me into one in the middle, and dropped the pizza boxes right on top of a haphazard pile of papers.

"Sorry about the mess. I wasn't expecting . . . anyone. But it always looks like this." He chuckled nervously, quickly running his fingers through his hair. He hadn't styled it today—or if he had, he'd worn the pomade right out of it with the nervous habit.

"So, this is your office," I prompted gently as I cracked open the box of garlic knots, and he passed me a paper plate from a desk drawer.

"This is it. Pretty drab, but the windows are nice." He gestured over his shoulder, and I walked around his chair to check out the view. It was sprawling, catching part of downtown Adele in the distance, and a good bit of gently rolling farmland beyond it.

"That is nice," I murmured, turning around to find him holding out a slice of pizza for me. "Thank you."

"Thank *you*, this looks way better than what I ordered. And quicker, too. You're an excellent delivery service. Gianni should hire you." He winked, and took a bit of gooey, cheesy pizza.

"Yeah, I don't think there's any chance of that happening."

"What, why?" His brow furrowed down, and I lowered myself into one of the chairs across from his desk.

"Uh, well . . . I ran into someone who wasn't happy to see me. And she got loud about it."

"Was it Suze? I thought you said she hadn't come back to town yet."

"Nope, I'm not sure—gosh, there's not a great way to bring this up. I think it was your ex-girlfriend? She was blond, nice tan. Drives a Prius. She didn't tell me her name, only . . . only that she'd get you back, and implied that I was a charity case." Embarrassment heated my cheeks, and I dropped my gaze to my lap to avoid his.

"Hey, whoa—whoa, whoa, whoa. You are not a charity case. That's absurd. If anything, I was. You rescued me from utter humiliation, and everyone knows it. Cindy—it sounds like Cindy—and I haven't dated for *years* and yet she still crops up every now and then on a tear. Honestly, I would have warned you if I thought she'd be so brazen to confront you in public. I am so sorry, Sienna." He sank into his chair, pizza forgotten as he dropped his chin into his palm on the desk. "This is so humiliating. I never dreamed—"

"Hey, it's okay, Finn." I reached across and laid my hand on his forearm, stopping him.

"It isn't. It really isn't, you didn't deserve to get waylaid by my ex unaware. I promise you we're not together, and haven't been together in a long, long time."

"So, you're not planning to toss me over and ride off into the sunset with her?" I grinned, trying to let him know he was off the hook.

"Absolutely *not.*" His look of horror made me laugh, right as a soft knock sounded on the side of his open door. One of his coworkers stood in the doorway hesitantly.

"Hey, uh, boss? Pizza's here. Although, it looks like you already found some."

"Thanks, Jorge. You guys go ahead and dive in."

"Aren't you going to introduce your lady-friend to the team?" Jorge waggled his eyebrows suggestively, and Finn's neck and ears turned red.

"Jorge, Sienna. Sienna, Jorge."

Jorge stepped into the office and offered me a hand, so I hastily swiped the pizza grease off my fingertips to shake it.

"Nice to meet you, Sienna. Where have you been hiding this one, boss?"

"I haven't been *hiding* anyone. We're taking our time." He growled, and a little shiver rocketed down my spine at the possessive tone, which was so rare for mild, friendly Finn. I *liked it. I liked it a lot.*

Jorge grinned, clearly enjoying ruffling Finn's feathers. "Nice to meet you, Sienna. If you get bored with him, give me a call." He winked, and Finn glared as he backed out of the room. "Easy, man—it's a joke."

Jorge winked at me and jogged off, probably to tell the rest of the team about *boss-man's* lady friend. I chuckled at his hasty exit, and the pained expression on Finn's face.

"Sorry about that," Finn said. "He thinks he's hilarious."

"It's fine. At least he's not causing a scene. Although, how does the gossip run around here? Anything like in town, or . . .?"

"Oh, the whole dev team will know in approximately two seconds. They might even take turns walking by, just to sneak a peek."

"So, same. Got it. Well, we'd better eat fast, then, huh, if we need to be ready for a close-up? Then I want you to tell me all about what it is you do." I gave him a devilish grin and stuffed a humongous bite of pizza in my mouth.

"Are you sure? Most people find it dull."

I nodded, swallowing my pizza. "I'm sure. This support thing is a two-way street. I want to know how you spend your time, too." I waggled my eyebrows and took another big bite, gesturing for him to do the same.

He returned my grin and followed suit.

Eleven

Rainy Days and Rainbows

Finn

A soft drizzle bathed the ground outside as I sat on my balcony finishing up a write-up on the issues this week for the VP board the following Monday. It wasn't scintillating, and I found myself frequently distracted. Frankly, it was a lousy way to spend a Friday night, and my mind kept wandering to Sienna. I'd texted her earlier, but no response. I checked my phone for the twelfth time, just to be sure, and there was still nothing. I plunked it down on the table and glanced up towards the creek. It wasn't much to look at from here, but my apartment building had nice shade from the trees, and I could hear the creek even if I couldn't see it from here.

I stared, blankly, my mind wandering until I saw a runner coming, despite the drizzle. She was keeping her eyes glued to the sidewalk, and wearing a bright purple raincoat covered in rainbows over her running gear. As she drew closer, I laughed, and shut the lid of my laptop. Standing up and crossing to the railing, I called out.

"Sienna? What are you doing running in the rain?" She jogged over, and looked up, making her hood fall back and reveal her bright purple hair twisted into a bun. Tendrils had broken free, framing her face haphazardly. She was utterly gorgeous, green eyes shining up at me.

"Hey, Finn. To be honest, I had to get out of the house. The office was tense—even Tamika, and she's *never* tense—and I just had to get out for a while. I was running my usual route, and then I thought I might swing by and see if you were home yet and say hi. It was only an extra two miles." She shrugged.

I rocked back on my heels, impressed by her athleticism. *Only* two miles—she was way out of my league, in a lot of ways. "Well, I'm glad you did. Are you done running? You can come in. I'll make you a cup of coffee to warm up, and we could order some dinner . . ."

"I'd like that, actually. Are you sure, though? This is twice I've randomly dropped by on you." She bit her bottom lip, and it hit me that she was feeling insecure.

"Sienna, I love it. I'm glad you're here. I texted you like an hour ago, and I've been pretending to work and daydreaming about seeing you again ever since." I gestured to my forgotten laptop, to underline the point.

"Oh, really? I didn't realize I'd been running that long, but I forgot my phone."

"That's okay. Do you want to come up?"

"Are you sure?" She fidgeted with the sleeve of her raincoat, and I nodded emphatically.

"Yes. Meet me around front?"

"Okay."

I gave her a quick wave, and then jogged through the apartment and down the stairs to meet her. I offered her a hand and led her up to my apartment. I pushed open the door and she stopped right inside to take off her dripping raincoat.

"I'll hang that up for you." I took the coat and hung it on a peg in the hallway, then pulled her into the kitchen. "Sit anywhere, and I'll start the coffee. Any preferences?"

"Uhm, strong? I'll drink it pretty much any way."
She shrugged and slipped onto a barstool.

"Strong, coming up!" I gave her a wink and went to work. While I wasn't a coffee nut like some, I could appreciate a good cup, and was confident I could make one she'd enjoy. Once the pot was started, I turned back around to face her, and caught her studying my apartment.

Her eyes snapped to mine, and a faint blush creeped up her neck.

"So, what's got you braving the weather to run?"

She dropped her chin into her palm, leaning on the counter. "I don't know, I was feeling suffocated at the office and the feeling followed me home. It gets like that sometimes when there's a new client. This one is the worst yet, though. They were supposed to pick two days ago and they didn't. Or they didn't pick us; I guess we'll find out eventually. But everyone's *tense*. And I would usually paint to get over it, but I didn't want the tension to flow out into the project." She looked down, tracing the pattern on the countertop with her free hand instead of meeting my eyes.

"Is it coming along well?"

"The painting?"

I nodded, and she nodded back, biting her lip again. "What is it? What's got you biting that lip?"

"Nothing, it's just . . . you really care, don't you?"

I stepped forward and propped my hip on the counter across from her, confused. "Of course I do. Why wouldn't I?"

"A lot of people think it's frivolous. My friends always ask what I'm working on, but at this point it's a challenge to see if I'll slip and tell them something. My family doesn't ask anymore, beyond what I'm doing at work. But . . . you're different."

"Is that a bad thing?"

"No, of course not. It's a really good thing, actually. I—I guess I'm starting to wonder how we've known each other so long and didn't wind up here before now." She gestured back and forth between us. "That probably sounds silly." She glanced up quickly, meeting my gaze and then dropping her eyes like the world's fastest game of tag.

I reached over, twining my fingers with hers and stopping the restless tracing. "I think people find each other when it's their time. No more, no less."

She squeezed my fingers in return. "Maybe so."

"*Definitely* so." She smiled at that, and I turned to pour her a cup of coffee.

"So, you're a talented, beautiful artist, an athlete, and you're sitting here, having coffee with me on a rainy Friday. How exactly did I get so lucky?" I passed her the cup, followed by a carton of half-and-half and some sugar.

She began doctoring the cup using precise, practiced movements. "I don't know; thank the rain. It soothes my asthma, and I always feel like I can run a little farther."

"Really? I didn't know you had asthma."

"Yeah, since I was a kid. It's typically well controlled, but every now and then it flares up. The rain helps; pollen doesn't. I've learned to deal with it." She gave her cup one final stir and took a tentative sip. Her eyes slid closed, and I couldn't help a smile.

"Good?"

"Incredible," she murmured, and took a second sip, and our eyes locked over the rim of the cup.

My throat tightened, and I had to resist the urge to pull her in my arms and kiss her. *She wants to finish her coffee, Finn. Settle down.* I cleared my throat, and forced out a simple, "Good," before turning to put the creamer and the sugar back away. Did my voice sound weird? I was overthinking it.

"So, uhm, want to watch a movie?" I stammered.

She lifted one corner of her lips in a small smile, and nodded, rising from her chair. "Do I get to pick this time, or are we watching another dinosaur movie?"

I snorted. "You can pick, but remember, movie mockery is also a two-way street." I nodded towards the living room, and led the way, suddenly anxious to know what she thought about my apartment. I lived alone, and I didn't have any of the beautiful art adorning the walls that she did. Was it stark? I didn't know. I stopped in front of the couch and stuffed my hands in the pockets of my shorts. "So, what are you in the mood for?"

"Definitely a Walk to Remember. It's classic."

"Isn't that the one where the girl dies at the end?"

She threw her head back and laughed. "Yes, but there's a lot of good stuff before that—it's romantic. *And* the perfect rainy-day movie."

"If you say so. I'm sure we can find it. Make yourself at home," I said, gesturing to the oversized couch and grabbing the remotes.

She pondered a moment and selected a spot on the chaise lounge, right at the back corner, and tucking her feet underneath her. Once she was settled, I slipped into the seat next to her, and began searching for the movie.

"Your place is surprisingly clean. I'm not sure if I've been misled about bachelor life by everyone, or if you're actually a super fastidious anomaly," she mused, glancing around at the half-empty shelves, freshly dusted and arranged.

"Neither, actually. I used to live with George—before he and Bea got married—and he kept up with all the cleaning. Once he moved out, things fell apart pretty quickly. I have ADHD and staying organized is difficult. My Aunt Dolly dropped by one afternoon and was *appalled.* After that I realized I needed help, so I hired a cleaner. Do you know Denise from Jude's? She comes by once a week and works her magic."

"Wow, I didn't know she cleaned. It looks really great."

"Yeah, she's starting her own business on the side."

"Are you and your aunt pretty close?"

"Yeah, decently so. My parents are off RVing around the country and enjoying retirement, so she and Uncle Steve are my only family here most of the time."

"Ahh. I overheard . . . well, Jenny and Marlie mentioned that you and your aunt might have gotten into it. About us." She held my gaze this time, the worry lines between her eyebrows like a punch to the gut.

"Ahh, it wasn't a big deal. She'd picked up on some gossip, and well . . . you know my aunt, she's all about appearances." I sighed, running my fingers through my hair restlessly. "She'll get over it as soon as the gossip blows over."

"Promise? I feel awful that I'm coming between you two. My relationship with my family is strained, and I really don't want to be the cause of that for you."

"Hey." I dropped my hand on her knee and ducked down to meet her eyes. "Look at me. I mean it. It's okay. You don't control the town grapevine. You didn't make her jump to conclusions. You did nothing wrong here. Heck, we did nothing wrong to begin with. This will blow over, and in a couple months everyone will be talking about what a cute couple we are and start taking bets when we're going to get married."

She froze, and I instantly regretted my joke about us getting married. I didn't want to spook her, I only wanted to take her mind off the town drama and my aunt.

"Are you okay? Please don't look like that. I feel like I just scared you to death."

"No, I—uhm . . ." She stopped, and looked at me with pure, unadulterated panic in her eyes.

"I freaked you out. It was a joke, I swear. A poor one, apparently. Please tell me what you're thinking, so I can fix whatever I broke right then. Please?"

"I hadn't thought about the long term. I know that sounds bad. I should, right? I'm the girl—I'm supposed to be the one hearing wedding bells, but I'm not that way. I'm never going to be that way. I don't—I should go. I'm sorry, Finn." She surged to her feet, and I leapt to my feet, too.

"Wait, Sienna, no. Please don't go." I reached out and put a hand on her arm, silently begging her to stay. She froze in her tracks, and I hurried to fill the empty silence hanging between us.

"I don't expect you to be hearing wedding bells. Not at all. This is all fresh, and I know that. I just—the town likes to jump to conclusions. George told me he and Bea hadn't been dating a month before every Granny in town started dropping hints. I promise, I was only trying to ease your fears about the gossip. Apparently, badly. Please, please don't go. If you'll tell me what's wrong, I promise never to say it again."

She turned to face me, and I could still see the concern in the way she drew her eyebrows down. The panicked look was gone, at least. "Finn, I wouldn't even know where to start explaining. It's not you, it's really me." She shrugged helplessly, and I carefully drew her back to the couch. She perched on the edge, her earlier ease gone.

"Start wherever you want."

She swallowed hard, and I could see the indecision on her face. She still looked like she might bolt for the door.

"If you tell me, I promise to watch your entire sad movie, and pretend it's romantic at the end." I made a lip-zipping motion. "No complaints whatsoever from here on out."

That brought a small smile to her face, and my spine relaxed a fraction.

"I'm not good with commitment." She flicked her eyes up to mine, clearly nervous about this line of discussion.

"Okay." I nodded, encouraging her to keep talking.

"My mom raised us alone. She married my dad before they even graduated high school, and the year after they graduated, she was pregnant with me. Well, *us*," she amended. "Their relationship wasn't ready to handle the strain of one kid, let alone two. My dad started drinking, they started fighting, and by the time I was three, he'd taken off. I don't know all of it—I was too young to remember, so I only know the bits and pieces my mom has complained about to me over the years when one of us bugged her enough for her to want to cuss him out for not being there to help."

"I can't imagine you being the cause of that often."

"It was usually Suze—not having a dad around made her act out. But I was the one standing by to hear the resulting rant from mom. And we struggled financially, of course. My mom did her best, but she was young and there were two of us." She looked down at her hands, fidgeting with the seam of the couch cushion. "So, commitment? It freaks me out. Getting married seems like a short path to a long, unpleasant road of heartache."

"Your mom never remarried?"

She shook her head, an aggrieved expression on her face. "No. She said she couldn't ever trust another man not to do the same."

"Wow, I'm sorry to hear that. I really stepped in it, didn't I?" I gave her my most apologetic smile, and she returned it briefly.

"It's okay. It's not your damage. You didn't know."

"I do now, though. And I do solemnly swear that there will be no more marriage jokes." I raised my right hand.

She huffed. "Oh, my word, was that a Harry Potter reference?"

"*Maybe*," I said innocently.

She lightly socked me on the arm and leaned back into the couch cushions. "I definitely won't be able to introduce you to Tamika. She'd try to steal you away. She loves Harry Potter; she's been to the theme park like *twelve* times."

"Now that's good taste." I grinned and leaned back against the cushions next to her. "Do you still want to watch A Walk to Remember? Because I do have all of the extended director's cuts of the Harry Potter movies. We could do a marathon."

She groaned and threw her arm over her eyes dramatically. "Is it even worth arguing with a Potter-head? Fine, we can watch them, but we're going to have to order Chinese food and I'm definitely going to steal more than my share of the wontons."

"Deal!" I grabbed my phone and dialed up Lee's Chinese.

Twelve

The Decision

Sienna

Monday mornings were never my favorite, given I had to leave my cozy art cocoon and head into the office. However, I found myself with some extra pep after spending so much of the weekend with Finn. It could have been a disaster—especially since I freaked out on him—but he always put me at ease. I'd never felt that way about anyone else, and the calm I'd found with him carried me like the remnants of a wave into the office Monday.

As soon as I sat down, I saw the notification; meeting in thirty minutes for the announcement on the new client. Nerves tightened like a noose around my stomach, and I instantly regretted my decision to have a double cup of coffee and skip breakfast. I had been calm, but that didn't mean I wasn't *bone-tired*.

I fired off responses to the few emails that had come in over the weekend, and then hightailed it to Tamika's desk. She was just coming in, with bags under her eyes and a leopard-print purse the size of an overnight bag slung over her shoulder.

"Morning, Tamika. Everything okay?" I asked, propping my chin on my hands at the top of her cubicle wall.

"Great, just great. Granny really needs a live-in aide, but I can't afford it so I've been spending the weekends with her, trying to catch up on all the stuff I can't do for her during the work week."

"Oh, Tamika. I'm so sorry. Can I do anything to help? What about Trevor?"

"No, uh-uh. I'm not calling Trevor. I have to figure out a schedule, that's all." She pursed her lips, angry at the idea of calling her estranged brother.

Seeing that it was pointless, I changed tactics. "Did you sleep at all this weekend?"

"Loads. I need a quick cup of coffee, and I'll be fine."

"Coffee I can do. You stay here, I'll grab us both a cup." I tapped the top of the wall, and pretended not to notice when she sighed, and slumped down to her elbows on the desk as soon as I turned away.

I was pouring the second cup in the breakroom and adding the five sugar packets Tamika preferred when Bryan came blowing into the breakroom and leaned on his forearm next to me on the counter. He was *always* crowding into my personal space, and I resisted the urge to stomp on his shiny shoes to get him to back up. Instead, I ignored him.

"Sienna, we need to chat."

"Really? I assumed you got winded on the way to the coffeemaker," I said drily.

"Ha-ha. Real comedian, aren't you?"

"Nope, just trying to caffeinate before the meeting." I pointedly dropped the crumpled packets into the trash can and began stirring. He did not take the hint.

"That's what we need to talk about. Sutherland called me."

I stiffened at the mention of his buddy who was one of the partner's sons but tried not to show it. *Please don't let Bryan have the account, please, please.*

"I'm sure we'll all hear in"—I checked my watch—"five minutes, when the meeting starts. Excuse me, I need to get back to Tamika with her coffee."

"Don't you want to hear what I know? I thought you might like a heads up."

"No thanks." I pushed through the door with my hip, and let it swing shut behind me. When I approached her desk the second time, Tamika was applying a light layer of powder on her nose, and all signs of her long weekend were gone.

"Here you go." I slid her the sugar-with-a-side-of-coffee and took the first sip of mine.

"You're the best, Sienna. I wouldn't survive this place without you," she murmured as she blew on her cup.

A pang of guilt hit me square in the chest. I was planning to use my hypothetical bonus to leave her, and she needed the money more than I did.

"How much does it cost to hire a night nurse, anyway? Would the bonus do it?"

"Girl, I wish. It might last a month, maybe six weeks? Even if I win, I still can't afford it. I might have to move in with her." She looked grim at the prospect. Tamika was vibrantly independent and loved living on her own.

"We'll figure something out. Maybe I can help?"

"I can't ask you to do that, Sienna. You've got your own life. This is my responsibility to figure out, and I will."

"Well, will you at least promise to tell me if you figure out something I can do? You shouldn't have to do this alone."

"You brought me coffee. Today, that's enough." She forced a wink and stood, so I dropped it. I didn't want to push, but I hated to see my friend struggling. If I got the bonus, maybe I could spare some to hire a cleaner for a while, at least? Surely that would help.

My phone vibrated in my pocket, and I pulled it out to see a message from Finn.

Finn: You've got this, killer. Knock them dead. *fist bump emoji*

I shook my head at his antics and trailed behind Tamika to the conference room as I tapped out a quick reply.

Sienna: Should I be concerned that you already think I'm a killer this early in the relationship?

Finn: Nope, consider it a throwback to my childhood soccer days. Put on your scary face!

With a snort I slid the phone back into my pocket and mused silently over Tamika's family situation while we took our seats in the conference room. Randy actually beat the crowd this time, while Bryan, Reese, and Lou came in on his heels.

As soon as they all found seats, Randy cut straight to it. "Thanks for coming, everyone. We've gotten a decision from Confectionary Delights, our newest client. Unfortunately, it's not cut and dried. They liked elements from two of the presentations, so the final project is going to be collaborative, which we didn't expect. However, one presentation has been chosen as primary, and that designer will be awarded the five-thousand-dollar bonus and acting lead role. The secondary contributor will receive an additional one thousand dollar bonus and have a supporting role on the project. Is everyone clear on that?"

My mind flashed back to Bryan approaching me in the breakroom, and my heart sank. *Did they pick me as secondary? Is that what he was trying to tell me?* It would be bad enough to get beat by Bryan, but to then have to play second fiddle to him while he adapted elements of my concept would be unbearable.

"Okay, then. Sienna, Bryan—" I held my breath, bracing myself for the bad news. "Your concepts were chosen. Sienna, you'll be lead. Congratulations, they loved the logo. Something about the watercolors mixed with their signature stripe? I'm sure they'll fill you in this afternoon. Bryan, your line-drawn concept—"

I didn't hear anything else he said, over the sound of blood rushing in my ears. I'd done it. *I'd done it.*

Tamika tapped me on the shoulder, breaking me from my reverie. "Way to go, girl. I knew it was going to be yours." She gave me a genuine smile, with not a hint of jealousy to be found.

"Thank you, Tamika. I'm really shocked."

Randy chuckled, and I realized that everyone in the room had gone quiet, staring at me. "Thank you, sir. I am really excited to get going on this project."

"You've earned it, Sienna. This will look great on your resume, especially if you decide to put in for the assistant art director position." He gave me a quick smile, rapped his knuckles twice on the table, and walked out.

Everyone shook my hand before leaving the room—even Bryan, who gave me a pointed look along with it—which I accepted, still in shock. There was only one thing on my mind as I left the room. I couldn't wait to tell Finn.

Thirteen

Belonging

Sienna

That night, Finn and I met up at the sushi place in town to celebrate my work victory. My head was still spinning with the client's project edits as I climbed out of my car at the restaurant, even though the meeting had ended nearly an hour ago. I closed my eyes and took two deep breaths, trying to step out of the stress and into date-mode. Once I finished, I smoothed down my dress. The bright green bodycon made my eyes pop, and I was kind of hoping that when Finn saw it his eyes would pop out. He was always such a gentleman, but it might be fun to ruffle him up a bit.

I bit my red-painted lip and scanned the sidewalk as I walked towards the entrance. It only took a moment, and a huge grin split his face when he spotted me. He waved with one hand, nearly upsetting the enormous bouquet clutched in the other. I sped up, eager to see him.

"Finn! You got me flowers!"

"You deserve it. Kicking the entire design team's *tails* to win the new client?" He leaned his head back and hollered, "My girl is a killer!"

A few guys clustered at the other end of the sidewalk hooted and hollered back.

"Finn!" I half-whispered. "You are crazy! Settle down." Heat rushed to my cheeks, evidence of the wild pumping of my heart at his enthusiasm. I put my hand on his arm to try to calm his over-the-top antics, but I wasn't angry. He was *proud* of me, and I loved every second of his goofy display.

He leaned forward and scooped me into a hug, the flower stems poking me in the back as he lifted me off my feet and spun me around. When we stopped, we were pressed chest to chest and I could feel both of our hearts beating wild, a matched set.

"I'm sorry, Sienna! I'm so happy for you. You deserved this, and now you can go after the next step with no reservations. That's worth making a ruckus over." He dropped his forehead down to mine, and time slowed around us as we simply breathed each other in, as tangibly mixed as the jasmine perfuming the night air.

When we stepped apart, it was only far enough for him to hand me the flowers and slip his arm around my shoulders. He held the door to the restaurant wide, and as I stepped through, the cool mist from the decorative waterfall washed over my exposed skin, leaving goosebumps up and down my arms.

The petite hostess directed us to a private booth in the back, and Finn waited patiently while I slid in, then took the bench across from me. We ordered, and then Finn leaned forward on his forearms.

"So, have you thought about it? Are you going to move forward with the art shop now?"

I shrugged one shoulder. "I'm not sure. I want to dive right in, but I got the schedule for finalizing the client's artwork, and it is tight. Even with what I already did, they want to incorporate some of Bryan's line work into my concept, which is going to take time. And they want a full branding package including custom art for a dozen different sizes of product containers. It's . . . a lot."

"Hmm. So, you'll be busy for a while?"

"At least six weeks, unfortunately. And if we don't stay on schedule, there will be overtime. Their deadline is firm."

"That does throw a wrench into things, but what if I helped? I know the guy who owns the building that's for rent over on Oak Street. If we negotiate, we could probably get you a month and a half free for build out, and that would give you time to order some stock, and set up the gallery area, right? I'd be willing to help nights and weekends to get it running."

"Finn, I don't know what to say. You've thought about this? It's a lot of work, and I haven't worked out yet how I'll staff the place until profits are able to cover my salary. I have a little bit set aside, yes, but . . . not a ton." I looked down at the table, embarrassed to discuss my finances. I didn't know why—*everyone* had bills to pay.

"Sienna, even if you start out only in the evenings, I know there would be plenty of town support for lessons. You were planning to do painting lessons for kids, right?"

"And adults," I agreed with a nod.

"Okay, well, they can't come during the day anyway. I'd be willing to wager the high school has a couple of eager art students who'd be willing to man a cash register in exchange for some free time in the art studio."

"That could work, actually. Open after school, and I could take over once I got back from the office."

"See? You can figure this out."

"I don't know anyone over at the school, though."

"Lucky for you, I do. And anyone we don't have a connection with, Aunt Dolly for *sure* does."

"You think your aunt is willing to help me, after the scene at the church last week?"

He grinned, the lopsided action highlighting a tiny dimple in his cheek. "Absolutely. I'll make it happen, one way or another."

Excitement welled up like a geyser, and I couldn't help but smile back at him. "Well then, I guess we should call the landlord, and see about a lease."

"He'll meet us at Sweet Nothings at eight. I already texted him."

My jaw dropped. "You were so sure I'd say yes?"

"No, but I hoped. If you'd said no, I'd have bought him a cup of coffee and introduced you two anyway." He shrugged, downplaying the amount of faith he'd put in my dream.

"Are you ever going to get tired of supporting me? Because honestly, some days it feels like you have more confidence in me than I do myself."

"One, never. Two, that's because you haven't realized how amazing you are yet. I've taken it as a personal challenge to get you to see your own worth."

Tears welled up in my eyes, and I blinked quickly to stuff them back down. I didn't quite manage it, and a single one escaped, making a break for it down my cheek. I looked down, hoping my hair would cover it and he wouldn't see.

"Hey, what's wrong? Did I overstep? It's your business, and I'll back down if that's what you want. We'll go at your pace, whatever that is. I—"

I was too choked up to speak, so I slid out of the booth. Panic rounded his eyes as he watched me, thinking I was walking out, but before he could stand, I slid in next to him and laid my head on his shoulder. He slipped his arm around me and tucked me under his chin. We sat in silence, and I worked on stopping the traitorous tears.

When I could speak again, it was softly. "Thank you, Finn. For believing in me. For pushing me. For seeing my dream as clearly as I see it myself. Don't ever stop, okay? I—" I swallowed hard, tears threatening to choke me again. "I didn't ever think I would find someone who understood. Who was proud of my art, proud of all of me. You're the only one who ever has been. Thank you."

"You don't ever have to thank me for being on your side. That's exactly where I belong," he murmured, rubbing my arm soothingly.

"Oh, well, isn't *this* precious."

My jaw dropped as I looked up from Finn's shoulder, and spotted his ex, Cindy, glowering at us with her hands on her hips.

"Cindy, what are you doing?" Finn's voice was low, the warning clear.

"What am I doing? Just being honest about how I feel, Finn. You think it doesn't hurt to see you here, cuddled up with another woman? We used to come here. I would still be here with you, if you opened your eyes to see that we're perfect for each other."

"Cindy, we came here *years* ago. We weren't perfect together; heck, we weren't even *happy* together. I'm sorry that you've had a hard time since we split, but it's time to move on. I have."

"With her? Seriously? The town *bohemian*?"

Why did everyone keep saying that like it was an insult?

She flicked her bleach-blonde hair over her shoulder, and glared at me. "What's so special about her? What does she have that I don't?" Her voice rose to a delirious pitch, and I winced at the shrill sound.

Finn leaned forward, an angry look on his face. "I am not doing this with you. Not now, not ever. You have to accept that it's over—it's *been* over for *years*—and leave Sienna out of this. I'm not going to sit here and compare the two of you. Now please, don't make a scene."

"This is ridiculous, Finn! You should leave her here, and come with me. You don't really want her, Finny. You don't. Say you don't!"

"Everything okay over here, folks?" Jesse Ferguson, town sheriff, drawled from over Cindy's shoulder. "I'm off duty, but I couldn't help but notice there seems to be a disagreement over here."

Cindy turned on him, indignant. "Everything is just fine, Jesse, and you should mind your own dang business!" while Finn said at the same time, "Everything is fine, Sheriff, Cindy was just leaving."

"Uh-huh," he said slowly, clearly having no trouble drawing conclusions about who the troublemaker was. "Why don't you come along with me, Cindy, and let these two lovebirds get back to their evening." He tipped his head towards me and Finn, as he took her by the arm.

We watched in numb silence as he resolutely led her towards the front of the restaurant, ignoring her protests the whole way.

"I am so sorry, Sienna. How humiliating," Finn said, dropping his head into his hands.

I reached over and rubbed his back soothingly. "Hey, it's all right. She's gone now, and everyone's already gone back to their meals. Look." He looked up, and I nodded at the few closest tables; every one of them was enjoying their evening, and the only woman still staring was craning her neck trying to catch a glimpse of Cindy, who was jabbing a finger into Jesse's chest at the front door.

"I know, but you hate drama, and I've dragged you smack into the middle of it. You know this is going to be above-the-fold gossip, by tomorrow." He pressed his lips together, clearly ashamed.

"Yep, it is. But you know what? You're worth it. And it will blow over. Celia was right about that."

"I'll make it up to you, somehow," he insisted.

"You don't have anything to make up for. But you heard the sheriff's orders—we've got to get back to our evening." I gestured for him to sit back up, and I leaned my head against his shoulder. "Does this seem to be about where we were?"

"Just about," he murmured, running his hand up and down my arm tenderly.

"Perfect."

"Yes you are." He placed a kiss on top of my head as the waitress arrived with our rainbow of sushi rolls.

The rest of the dinner passed in an uninterrupted glow of time well spent and good conversation. All the while, we stayed there, tucked together, without any other place we'd rather be, even if our small town was a little bit crazy.

Fourteen

Shopaholic

Sienna

After our night of sushi, everything around me seemed to speed up. Work kept me running, every day from the moment my eyes opened, to the moment they closed over the next six weeks.

Finn and I met with Greg, the landlord for the little shop on Oak Street. With Finn at my side, we negotiated two full months of rent abatement to set up shop, in exchange for giving his middle daughter Maggie art lessons for six months on Saturdays once I was up and running. He promised to spread the word to all her other friends' parents, too.

So not only did I have a shop, but I had my first student. Each day was a hectic cycle of running to the office early to work on the Confectionary Delights account, watching my vision blossom across their product line, dealing with Bryan's sulking, and zipping out the door the minute my last meeting ended to head to Oak Street. Finn met me every single evening, and even pulled in a host of his town friends to help me make the shop perfect.

George, his former roommate, helped design a layout for the building where I had shelving for supplies, as well as a gorgeous gallery room, and a separate classroom at the back. There was even a coffee nook, which I was especially proud of.

Finn helped me paint on the weekends, assemble shelving units, and start placing stock in the store. Another week, he called in two of the Ferguson brothers to install custom lighting in the gallery, so each painting had a spotlight, as well as a chandelier in the center to add a touch of elegance.

Jenny and Marlie had brought us late night pizza more than once and stayed to help stock shelves and set up easels in the classroom. Marlie mostly put her feet up and offered opinions, but I appreciated all the moral support they had given through the process, not once complaining that "girls' nights" had become volunteer work nights.

Even his aunt Dolly—who still wasn't sold on me yet—had started hauling her friends in on the odd evening to show off the space and see about hosting ladies' painting events. I was incredibly surprised by that, but hopeful that I might be able to pay the graduated lease payments, even without being open all day every day. When she left, she kissed Finn on the cheek, and patted me on the shoulder.

I decided not to look *that* particular gift horse in the mouth and said a quick prayer of thanks that she seemed to be coming around.

By week six of preparations, I was utterly exhausted, still in need of a point-of-sale system and coming down with a cold. Too much work, not enough sleep. But we were so close to the finish line, I couldn't stop yet. We'd set a soft opening date in two weeks, and to celebrate I was putting together an art expo with pieces from myself and other local Adele artists. I had big plans for showing Finn the painting I'd nearly completed—the one I'd started at the beginning of our relationship.

It was Friday night, and Finn and I had plans to hang the first few gallery pieces. He was installing the hardware, and I was selecting items from my personal collection to get things started. Though really, all I wanted to do was eat soup and fall into bed.

The door was already unlocked when I arrived, and his truck was parked out back with some long trim pieces hanging out the back. I pushed through the back door—smiling at the beautiful lettering I'd had printed and applied to the employee's entrance—and called out for Finn.

"Hey, I'm here. I know we have a lot left to do, but I think tonight might have to be an early one. Honestly, I'm starting to feel worn down." I stopped, realizing all was quiet. "Finn? Where did you go?"

"I'm in the gallery! Come on in," he called.

I dragged my feet on the way, running my hands over the beautiful, burnished-wood shelving full of canvases.

"Did you already get started?" I asked as I rounded the corner, and my jaw nearly fell to the floor.

"Surprise!" Finn threw his arms wide and spun around, leading me to take in all the work he'd done. The last of the lighting was up, the hardware was all in, and a cluster of balloons were tied to a stool in the center of it all. He'd even turned on one of the spotlights and hung his favorite charcoal bench piece underneath it.

"Finn, it looks great in here! I can't believe you did all of this. You didn't leave anything for me," I added guiltily.

"It's all done. All you have left to do is hang the pieces and the price tags. I think, my lovely Sienna, you've more than earned a night off." He crossed the space and patted the stool.

I walked over to him and sank into his waiting arms, forgoing the seat. "Are you even real?"

He let out a startled laugh and planted a kiss on the top of my head. "What do you mean? Of course, I'm real."

I sighed, and leaned back, looking up into his handsome face. Finn had no idea how spectacular he was, and after how much he'd been here for me through all of this craziness, there were no doubts whatsoever left in my mind how committed he was to me.

He had a five o'clock shadow today, and I ran my fingertips gently over the rough stubble. "You are, aren't you? You're real, and you're mine."

"Yes I am," he murmured, dropping a sweet kiss onto my waiting lips. When we pulled apart, I dropped my head back onto his chest, my ear picking up the sweet, soothing sound of his heartbeat. "Now, sit your cute self down on that stool, and tell me where you want the art." He waggled his eyebrows at me ridiculously, and then crossed the room to pick up the first piece.

"I already hung the bench, but we can move it if you want. This is the weird one, with the black and white nose." He turned the large charcoal drawing towards me.

"Ahh, yes. Bernard submitted that. I was thinking that side." I pointed to the spot, and he walked over.

"Bernard from the fire department?" he asked as he hung it up.

"The one and only. Well, unless you count his great uncle who he was named after."

"Huh, well. It's very . . . large."

I snorted. "You don't have to like all of the pieces. They just have to be cohesive."

"Well, I like all of yours. Does that count?"

"Absolutely."

"Okay, next up we have . . . whatever this is."

"It's abstract."

"Sure, let's call it abstract. Where do you want it?"

"Are you sure you don't want me to help you hang them? It would go twice as fast."

"I'm sure. You sound exhausted, and this is something I can do."

"Okay then, across from the nostril, next to the window."

"Yes ma'am," he drawled, and hauled the large, splatter-colored piece across and hung it. We still had some work cut out for us, but we were very nearly there. For the first time in a long time, I was full. Of hope, excitement, and—not that I would admit it yet, even to myself—*love*.

Fifteen

Hunker Down

Sienna

The night we hung the paintings was the last night I was able to work on the shop for three whole days. My sniffles turned into a full-on plague beast of a cold, and I spent the time curled up in my house, online ordering last-minute needs for the shop in between sipping soup and watching trashy tv. It wasn't much, but I survived. Finn called me multiple times a day to check in, and it took all the energy I had left to keep him away, so he didn't catch my cold.

He was stubborn in the best ways, that man. By Tuesday I was still tired, but at least able to get back into the office so I could oversee the final touches on the Confectionary Delights project. It had turned out beautifully, and even I had to admit that Bryan's details added a great contrast to what I'd originally put together.

I'd barely sat down at my desk when he poked his head over the cubicle wall.

I looked down at my watch. "You should not look that angry at seven-thirty in the morning. It can't be good for you."

He rolled his eyes. "Where have you been? We are in crunch time, and you called out yesterday like it's nothing? Don't think word hasn't gotten around about your *personal project*. Don't you think that's a conflict of interest, taking a day off to work on that when your deliverables aren't complete here?"

Great, now I was angry at seven-thirty in the morning. "Listen, Bryan, I don't know what you've heard, but I spent the entire weekend holed up in my house, trying not to spread germs. I'm still stopped up, in case you couldn't tell over the sound of your own voice. I would *never* jeopardize things here by calling in sick if I wasn't actually sick. Now, how are the product stickers coming along?"

"Fine," he ground out through clenched teeth. The '*no thanks to you*' was implied.

"Great, thanks for handling that. I'll review them first thing, and we'll go from there." I popped a cough drop into my mouth and gave him the *go away now* look.

He pursed his lips but took the hint and left. My shoulders sagged, tired from even the small confrontation. I really wanted to do nothing but go back to bed, but it simply wasn't an option. I had taken two days of vacation to handle the shop's launch the following week, which meant my work project had to be out the door before then.

I shook it off and got to work.

Tamika stopped by my desk at two o'clock, a concerned look on her face.

"I'm fine," I said mulishly before she even said a word. "I've got too much to do to spend another workday in bed. We're close, though, and then I can catch up on rest."

"Well, I'm glad to hear that, but I'm not here to mother you—this time, anyway." She squinted at me, like she suspected I was exaggerating how fine I was. "I'm here to tell you to go home. Didn't you see your email?"

"Uhm, no? I've been resizing sticker designs. What's the email?"

"It's from Randy's secretary. The tropical storm has changed course, and they're closing the office early so people can go home and batten down the metaphorical hatches. Although Randy *has* a boat, so there might be literal battening. TBD on that one." She tapped her chin in speculation. "Regardless, pack up and we'll walk out together."

I resisted a groan. "Tamika, I have so much to do. There's not really anything to do at home besides hit the grocery store for water and batteries."

She leveled a stare at me. "What are you planning to eat if the power goes out?"

"I already live on Pop Tarts. I went to Costco last week—I'm ready for an apocalypse of up to . . ." I did the mental math. ". . . three weeks. I even have canned soup left from my germ-infested weekend."

She rolled her eyes. "Too bad, the office is literally closing around you. Even Bryan ran like half an hour ago, and the facilities guy can't lock up until we skedaddle."

I looked around, and sure enough she was right. Other than us, there was only the facilities manager Rob and one other employee, already heading for the door. I had really zoned out.

"Okay, okay, I'm hurrying." I shoved everything I needed into my purse, and the two of us made for the door at lightning speed, waving to Rob on the way out. He gave us a cursory salute and locked up before heading back to turn off all the lights.

The wind was blowing sideways when we came out, catching my skirt and making me bump into Tamika. "Are you sure this is only a tropical storm? I haven't checked the news." I had to raise my voice to be heard over the wind.

"I don't know. That's what it was last I checked, but this feels strong for a tropical storm. It could be strengthening, if these are the outer bands."

"Great, just great," I muttered. "Okay, well, drive safe and text me a bunch." We exchanged a quick side hug, and then charged off to our cars, leaning into the whipping wind.

No sooner was I on the road than I got a call from Finn.

"Hey, Finn."

"Hey, Si-si. Have you been keeping an eye on this storm?"

"No, but the office is closed and I'm heading home now. What about you?"

"Well, I was sent home, too. With my laptop, to work until the Wi-Fi gives out," he said drily.

"Lucky you."

"Yeah. Hey, do you need any supplies? We could go out and brave the masses together."

I mulled it over. I didn't need much—it was easy to supply a single person—but, one more Finn outing before we had to lock down for the storm could never be a bad thing.

"Sure, I could always use an extra case of water."

"Pick you up in an hour?"

"Sounds good. See you then."

"Drive safe, Si."

"You too, Finn."

Finn knocked on the door precisely an hour later, and I was ready. Rain boots, rain jacket, and purse tucked under my arm, I locked up quickly and we headed for his truck.

"You think it's going to rain already?" he asked as he held the door for me.

"Maybe? I'm not sure how long the calm will last before *this* storm. I looked it up, and it's now a category two. So, we could be in for some bad weather sooner than later."

He nodded, went around to his side and climbed in. "Ehh, I'm sure it will be fine. I don't worry unless it's more than a three."

"Me either, actually. Does that make us weird?"

"Nope, you should hear the Floridians. They're all heading for Disney World right now," he joked as we headed for Publix. "So, are you ready for the soft opening next weekend?"

"Yeah, honestly I am. *We* are. I've made up some invitations to hand-deliver, and I also posted it on some virtual small business boards, and a couple flyers in the key gathering spots around town."

"Using those extraordinary design skills, as always." He looked over at me with a grin, then squeezed my hand. "I know it's going to be great. The shop is beautiful. What's left?"

"Not much, thanks to you and your cadre of connections. About ninety percent of the stock is already in place. I've got a few more easels that I'm waiting to get delivered for the classroom, some more sample projects I want to complete and hang in there, and a few late supplies that will go on the shelves. Worst case scenario, I can shift things around for a couple days so there aren't any empty spots on the displays."

"Sounds like a solid plan. Anything else I can help with?"

"Not unless you've got some magical anti-jitter pill. I swear, the closer we get, the more nervous I get. I'm excited, sure. But this is a big deal, and we've done so *much* in such a short amount of time. Although, I'm glad of that now that the storm is coming. I'd be stressed if we still had major renovations to do with the bad weather causing delays."

"Yeah, it worked out, didn't it?"

"It really did." I gave him a warm smile and rubbed the back of his hand. He pulled into a space near the back of the lot, which was cram packed. People buzzed in and out of the store, heads down and casting wary glances at the overcast sky. Our normally garrulous town had been reduced to quick waves as we all prepped for the impending storm.

Finn and I both hopped out at the same time, and linked arms as we headed inside. I grabbed one of the last three available carts as his phone rang.

"Hey, Aunt Dolly. Uh-huh, we just walked in. Yes, we. Sienna is here. Do you need anything while we're here? Okay. Uhm . . ." He cast an apologetic glance my way before putting his hand over the microphone and whispering, "Do you mind if we pick up a few things for them?"

I shook my head and gave him a thumbs up.

"Sure, text me the list. I'll grab it for you. Okay, wow. Okay, well, I've got to—" He closed his eyes briefly, then tried again. "Okay, send me the list but I've got to go if I'm going to get everything before it's sold out. All the buggies are already gone, and you know what *that* means. Okay, bye."

He hung up, and I shook my head. "She is a talker, huh?"

"Yeah, you could say that again."

"Nah, I'll leave that to Dolly. So, what do you need?"

He chuckled. "Not too much. Water if they've got it, and some batteries for my backup power pack. Gotta be able to charge my phone."

"Err, you may have missed the boat on both of those, but we'll see."

He shrugged. "Well, let's get to it."

An hour later we emerged with a buggy full of items for Aunt Dolly, and an off-brand pack of AA batteries successfully in tow.

We made it halfway back to his truck when the rain started, dark clouds looming from the east.

"Ugh, here it comes! This one feels sudden," I complained as I pulled up my hood. "We usually get more warning before it's on top of us."

"You were sick all weekend and missed the news. They've been giving this one a lot of airtime, saying it had the potential to escalate. Although they *always* say that. I was counting on them being wrong again."

We quickly chucked all of the groceries and supplies in the back seat before climbing in. He tried to hold my door for me, but I waved him off since the rain was picking up. As we got settled, a chill ran up both of my arms from the sudden temperature drop.

"Do you want me to drive you home first? Or would you like to ride with me to Aunt Dolly's? Get a few more minutes together, before the storm."

"Definitely a few more minutes. I missed you this weekend."

He lifted my hand, our fingers still twined together, and kissed the back of my knuckles. "I missed you too. I'm glad you're feeling better."

"Thanks. Me too," I murmured, and we both slipped into silence as he concentrated on navigating the truck safely through the nasty weather.

SIXTEEN

Hurricane

SIENNA

The supply drop at Dolly's was surprisingly quick, and she even waved at me from the porch while Finn carried their supplies in through the rain. After that, Finn drove me home and helped me unload my few last-minute supplies. He even carried my water bottles into the pantry for me and didn't laugh at my enormous box of Pop Tarts. He didn't even complain about getting soaked, and his shirt was sticking to him like glue by the time we made it inside my house.

While he was in the pantry, I slipped off to the hall closet to grab him a towel.

He accepted it with an appreciative smile. "Thank you."

"You're welcome. Thank *you* for driving, and helping me carry things in. Can I fix you a cup of coffee? Warm you back up?"

He glanced out at the churning storm, but nodded anyway. "I'd love a cup, if you don't mind the company."

"Your company? Never." I gave him a wink, then went about the business of making him a cup.

Once the elixir of life was ready, we took our cups out on the back porch, and cozied up on the porch swing. We swung gently and sipped our coffees in comfortable silence as the storm slowly built around us. His arm was wrapped around my shoulders, and I had my feet tucked up underneath me. If it weren't for the hurricane, I would wish for that moment every single day.

What would it be like, if we really *were* together every day? I'd told him I was afraid of commitment—and I stood by that—but this boy was putting *forever* thoughts in my head on an almost daily basis. I was a big old conundrum on two legs. What was wrong with me?

Eventually, a huge branch of lightning lit the darkening sky, and we ambled inside.

"I should probably head home before it gets any later. Don't want to push it too far, driving in this mess."

"Call me when you get there, so I know you're safe?"

"Absolutely." He leaned in for a kiss, and I closed the distance between us happily. I walked him to the door and watched as he backed the big truck out of my driveway, and as his taillights were swallowed up by the storm a few moments later. All the while, I wished he didn't have to go.

Bzzz, bzzz.

Bzzz, bzzz.

I rubbed my eyes and blinked up at the ceiling in confusion.

Bzzz, bzzz.

Was that my alarm? No, wait. There was still a big storm happening outside. I could turn it off. I reached over and slapped my hand on the phone, but after a moment of blissful silence, it started up vibrating again.

With a groan, I propped myself up on one elbow to see why it hadn't shut off.

Three missed calls from Suze.

I groaned again—for an entirely different reason, this time—and considered lying back down. It was only—three in the morning. Nothing good came from answering Suze's calls before dawn. Not once.

And yet, the wind wailed against the side of the house, the rain coming down sideways against my bedroom window, and suddenly I was wide awake.

I sat up, brushed my purple hair out of my face, and dialed Suze back.

"Took you long enough," she snarled when the call connected.

"Oh, I am so going back to bed. Don't call me again until after seven—I'm turning this phone off."

"Wait! I need help!" I heard her shout as my finger hovered over the red button.

I closed my eyes briefly, pinching the bridge of my nose in frustration as I lifted the phone back to my ear.

"What kind of help could I possibly give you at three in the morning?" I groused.

"I need you to pick me up. Billy left me at a truck stop last night. I haven't been able to get a ride, because everything's down for the storm. You're it, Sienna. I need you to come get me."

"A truck stop? And who's Billy?"

"It's a long story, okay? Can you just come get me?"

"Suzanne, it's in the middle of the night, and a category two blowing outside. I cannot drive anywhere right now. If you've been there all night, aren't you safe a couple more hours until the sun comes up at least? I will come get you, but—" Lightning cracked outside, and I jumped, clutching my pajama top as if it would defend me.

"Sienna, I wouldn't have called you if I wasn't desperate. The power went out here five minutes ago, and the owner is saying everyone has to leave because the security system went down. Please, I can't go out in this, and I can't stay unless I have a ride coming. *Please.*"

"Okay. Okay, I'm coming. Where are you?" I grabbed a notepad from my nightstand, and quickly scrawled down the name and address of the truck stop over in Macon. "Hang tight, and I'll be there as soon as I can."

She hung up without saying thank you, and I hauled myself out of bed. I walked into the bedroom and flipped the light switch, with no response. *Perfect.*

Fifteen minutes later I was in my car, rain boots on over my pajama pants, a raincoat and a stack of towels in the passenger seat, heading two hours due west to a shady truck stop, also without power. I took it as slowly as I could as the road wound out of town, even the familiar drive sketchy in the dark with the high winds.

I bit my lip and concentrated on keeping track of the yellow center lines through the dumping rain, with nothing to distract me but the endless drone of the weather radio channel, and the wind howling and beating up against the sides of the car.

My knuckles were tight on the wheel as I drove, and a few minutes in I was out of familiar territory and seriously questioning my decision to pick her up in the middle of the night. Surely there was a shelter nearby? A red light loomed ahead, and I picked up my phone to send her a message asking if there was a shelter she could get to, when it flashed low battery.

Ugh. No power on at home, so no overnight charge. I took advantage of the empty intersection and stayed put with my flashers on while I dug around for a charge cord . . . which I'd taken out last week when I took my car to the wash. Shoot, that was not good. What if I got stuck, and needed to call 911?

I sat there another long minute, torn. I didn't want to do something stupid and get stuck with no way to call for help. But I also didn't want to abandon Suze to a dangerous situation. I was already more than two hours away, with how slow I was having to drive. I made a decision and shot off one last quick text.

I turned off my phone to save the last bit of battery and started back down the road.

I was over halfway there when I hit a major road-block. A bridge I needed to go over was closed, and I was waved away by the police officer parked at the end. When I stopped, unsure where to go next, he walked over to my car, hanging onto the brim of his raincoat's hood to keep it somewhat over his face in the gale.

"Ma'am, you need to go home immediately. This is unsafe weather, and the bridge is closed."

"I'm really sorry, officer. I'm trying to get to Macon. My sister's in trouble, or I would be at home still asleep. Is there any other way around? She's counting on me to pick her up."

He flattened his lips, clearly unsure whether to help me, or send me back the way I came.

"I promise you, as soon as she is safely in my car I will drive straight home. Please, officer."

He shook his head slowly and gave me terse directions before jogging back across to the shelter of his squad car.

I was tired, it was late—early?—and I was not great with directions. Hopefully my car's GPS would catch up, if I stuck close enough to the route he'd given me. It was only a few turns, and a few road names. I could do this.

I kept driving cautiously, eyes peeled for the roads he'd told me, and I found the first two without trouble. The third was only supposed to be "a few miles" further, but I glanced down at my odometer and it said I'd already been five. Five slow, creeping miles of nothing but trees and blackness surrounding the thin beams of my headlights.

Another blast of wind hit me broad-side, and I jerked the wheel left to keep it on the road, blowing out a shaky breath. This was not going well, and I still had half the trip to go.

I took another deep breath in and out through my nose to stay calm, and kept driving. Worst case scenario, I could turn around and go back to that bridge with the officer.

After another mile, my GPS suddenly updated to the new route, and it advised a right turn at the next road.

"Praise the Lord, and pass the fried chicken," I muttered hoarsely as I turned onto the elusive road. Wainwright. Had that been the road he'd given me? I was starting to question, but the GPS said the route was the same distance as before. Good enough for me.

The asphalt quickly turned to gravel, followed by unpaved, washboard dirt, forcing me to slow even further. Water ran in thick rivulets down either side of the road, and I found myself drifting towards the middle since there was no shoulder. I did *not* want to slip off into the muck and get myself stuck. That would really knock the perfection of this evening up a notch.

The road narrowed, the water on either side accumulating into small streams, all running the same direction as I was. My nerves grew as two lanes shrunk to one and a half, and the ruts in the road grew thicker. I hadn't passed any houses since I'd turned off, and the GPS showed three more miles on this road before the next turn.

I reached up and turned off the radio, as the constant repetition was making me itch. Around the next bend, a tiny, flat bridge spanned a swollen creek, and I hit the brakes. The streams of water running on both sides of me gushed in to join the larger body of water, splashing upward as they met and creating tiny whitecaps.

There were guard rails on the bridge, and their yellow reflectors bounced back my headlights, showing that even the bridge had water up over the edges.

I couldn't do it. Driving onto that bridge would be beyond stupid because the water was clearly rising. The rain hadn't stopped, which meant the water level hadn't stopped either. I craned forward in my seat, trying to figure out how to get out of the mess. There was no room to turn around, so I would have to try to carefully back down the narrowed road until I could turn without sinking my tires into the water.

I put on my flashers once again and slid the shifter into reverse. *You can do this, Sienna. You can back up perfectly fine. All you have to do is ignore the wind, and the water on both sides, and take it slow. No big deal. No big deal, no big deal.*

I chanted it to myself as I carefully stepped on the gas, eyes glued to the rearview mirror. The car rocked back, and then stopped. I held my breath and tried again, pushing a little harder this time. A weird sound broke through the insistent rain, like pellets whacking the underside of the car.

"What in the heck?" I looked down through my side window and had to close my eyes to stop the instant onslaught of tears. "No, no, no! I cannot be stuck." I smacked my palm on the steering wheel in frustration. "I cannot be stuck next to this overblown creek in the middle of nowhere!" I leaned my head back against the headrest for a moment and looked up at the ceiling of the car. "I was careful. So *careful*. There has to be a way out of this. I just need to stay calm and figure it out. Think, Sienna. You've seen people stuck on the side of the road before. How did they get out?"

Time slowed to a crawl as I tried every maneuver I could think of to get the wheels unstuck. Cutting to both sides and trying the gas—carefully, so I didn't dig a bigger hole—felt like it helped, but in the end the tires rocked back down into the same spot, only closer to the stream on the right side of the car. And was that stream getting bigger, or was that my imagination playing games with me?

If I had a shovel, I could try digging my way out, but I didn't have anything in the trunk to use. One last look at the water— which, yep, it was definitely encroaching—sent me scrambling for my phone, as that familiar tightness rose in my lungs.

I turned it back on, praying for a miracle that someone would be close enough to come get me before I had to abandon my car and try to walk back up the road in this soup, while my lungs protested the whole way.

The screen turned on and immediately dimmed, flashing the same low battery warning as before. That wasn't the bad part, though. When I saw the bleak *no signal* error flashing on the top of the phone, the tears I'd been holding back began to fall, and I gave up on trying to stop them.

Seventeen

Gut Check

Finn

I couldn't say what exactly woke me, only that I went from a dead sleep to high alert in an instant. At first I brushed it off as the weather and rolled over to go back to sleep. Something deep in my gut, though, wouldn't let me. Five minutes later I gave up trying and sat up in bed with a sigh. If I was going to be awake, I could at least watch TV as long as the power lasted. I fumbled around on the nightstand in the dark for the remote and bumped my phone.

It lit up brighter than the fourth of July and made me wince, until I saw a notification from Sienna. I snatched it up, squinting at the brightness as I read her message.

Sienna: Hey Finn, Suze called and she's in trouble. I'm heading to pick her up. Address below. Phone is almost dead, but I'm going to turn it off in case I need to make an emergency call. Just wanted someone to know where I went. Hope you're sleeping well and see this in the morning when we're already home. XOXO, Sienna.

The time stamp read forty-five minutes ago, and without thinking it through, I threw my legs over the side of the bed and was on my feet. She said she'd turned off her phone, but I called anyway, in case she'd found a charger.

It went straight to voicemail, and I cussed a blue streak. After the fastest pit stop known to mankind in the bathroom, I shoved my feet into boots from the back of the closet, threw on a raincoat, and grabbed the truck keys. If she was driving all the way to Macon in this weather, I would be hot on her heels.

I made decent time, and besides the wind which kept trying to pull me sideways, the trip was uneventful until I got to a downed bridge.

The cop was angry when he climbed out of the car, and I braced myself for a ticket. Frankly, if it said, "being too stupid to function, driving in this weather," I wouldn't have blamed him. It *was* nasty out. The time probably didn't help his mood, either.

He muttered under his breath as I rolled down the window.

"Two idiots in twenty minutes. What is wrong with people tonight?"

"Did someone else just come by?"

He narrowed his eyes at me underneath the bright yellow hood of his raincoat. "Yeah, two soakings for me. Now, go home."

"Sir, I got a message from my girlfriend that she was going to pick up her sister. I need to make sure she gets there safely. Her car is small. I wish she'd told me she had to drive somewhere—my truck is a lot safer in these conditions."

He let out a weary sigh, and quickly rattled off directions. I thanked him profusely as he turned and trotted back to his car and out of the weather.

Knowing I was on the right track, I pushed the speed as fast as I comfortably could without missing the road signs.

When his instructions sent me down a slush-pit of a dirt road, I groaned. There wasn't a single tire track on the road ahead of me. Either Sienna had seen how nasty this road was and turned around, or she'd gone another way. I supposed it was possible the rain had already washed away the tracks, but . . . if she'd turned around, wouldn't the officer have seen her and told me?

I threw the truck in park and mulled it over. If I turned around now, I'd spend the entire night worried until she called. I picked up my phone, and before I could dial her yet again—all my prior attempts had gone to voicemail—the phone flashed "Out of service area." That was par for the course, wasn't it? Technology always failed at the most inopportune times.

I rubbed the back of my neck idly as I thought on it. When I finally came to a decision, I reversed back onto the pavement, and decided to keep driving a little longer. If I checked the next few roads and found a paved one, I'd try it. If not, well, I'd cross that particular bridge when I got to it.

I kept my eyes peeled, but there were no more roads for a couple of miles, and I began to second-guess my decision. Driving along hoping to catch her trail sounded fine at the time, but why didn't I check that first road beforehand? The rain was still coming down; it could have washed away her tracks. My right hand was fisted, bouncing on my thigh as I drove and mentally berated myself for not having a better plan of attack when I spotted another road.

It was also dirt, and I sucked in a breath as my headlights revealed a semi-faded set of tire tracks. Without hesitation, I followed them.

The road was rougher than a cob, and I found myself shifting forward on the truck seat, trying to ease some of the bumping. It didn't work, but I was tense as the truck's shocks utterly failed to ease the way, and my head was bouncing off the ceiling.

There was a curve up ahead, and the road was already less than a single lane wide with all the water pouring down the shoulders. Surely, *surely*, Sienna hadn't tried to take this road. This had to be a local, or a four-wheeler, or somebody out storm chasing.

When I cleared the curve, I slammed on the breaks and skidded to a stop in the thick muck. There it was, her little sedan. Mud flecked the sides, and my heart hammered in my chest at the sight of it, not a foot from a flooded river, and water underneath the car. I didn't stop to think or grab my raincoat, just threw the truck into park and dove out feet first.

The thick mud sucked at my boots, but I managed to keep them on as I hobbled the short distance between our vehicles. *Please God, let her not have tried to walk off in this. Please God, let her be okay.* The words of a silent prayer ran together in my head as I covered my eyes to block the rain and tried to see if she was still inside. The window began to roll down, and I breathed a sigh of relief as I drank in her gorgeous, tear-stained face.

"Sienna!"

"Finn? What—what are you doing here? Oh my gosh, I'm so glad you're here!" She choked on a sob, and my heart tried to rip itself in half.

"Come on, get out of the car. We've got to get out of here." I reached for the door handle, single-minded on getting her safely out of a dangerous situation. The water flirted with my ankles, and I was glad I'd thrown on my old cowboy boots, not my usual pair of weekend tennis shoes.

She reached behind her to the other seat for her things, and as soon as she had what she needed in hand, I scooped her out of the seat, pushed her door shut with my knee, and started slogging back towards the truck without setting her down. The headlights showed the black water swirling with mud as I trudged through it, Sienna cradled against my chest. I opened the door, careful not to drop her, and slid her into the seat ahead of me. She scooted across the bench to make room for me, and I climbed in behind her.

I turned sideways in the seat so I could see her. My heart pounded and my chest heaved, adrenaline pumping through me like I hadn't felt before. She pressed a towel into my shaking hands, and I took it numbly.

"Are you okay? Did you wreck, or get stuck? I should probably know that. Do you need a doctor?" I ran a hand through my hair, causing rivulets of water to run into my eyes and down the collar of my shirt. Belatedly, I rubbed the towel over my hair to sop some of it up.

"No, I didn't wreck. I saw how narrow the bridge was and tried to back up down the road to turn around, but the wheels got stuck. I'm fine. I was scared, but you found me before anything worse could happen, I— How did you find me? I tried to call as soon as I realized I was stuck, but the phone has no service." She held up a useless, dead cell phone to illustrate the point.

"Your text. As soon as I saw it, I jumped in the truck." I watched as she ran a second towel—had she brought those along?—over her arms, and shivered in the seat. Without thinking, I reached for the dials and turned on the heat. A particularly strong gust wailed against the side of the truck, and I threw it in four-wheel low and began backing down the mud pit of a road.

"Thank you," she murmured, meeting my gaze after wrapping the damp towel around her shoulders.

"You're welcome."

"Not just for the heat. I mean, thank you for that, too. You're always considerate." She paused, staring blankly out the front window as her car grew further and further away, the water nearly to the bottom of the door, now. "Thank you for coming. It was terrifying, and I feel so *stupid*." She reached up and scrubbed one of her eyes with the heel of her hand. "I thought I was being cautious enough, but I couldn't leave Suze. She annoys me to death, but she's family. Blood."

I spared a quick glance her way as I continued backing down the road and saw a fresh track of tears starting down her cheeks.

"Hey, it's okay. You're not stupid. The only thing you did wrong was not waking me up and taking me with you. My truck can get us there."

"What? Aren't we going home?"

"We can if that's what you want, but doesn't she still need to be picked up?"

She nodded hesitantly.

"Then we'll find another way around. We have to get off this road first and get somewhere with a cell signal and report your car, too, while we're on the way."

"Oh, right. It's probably going to be flooded by morning when we can get it out of there." She leaned her head against the passenger door and closed her eyes. Exhaustion seemed to weigh down her shoulders, and I wanted nothing more than to take all the stress away. I couldn't take it all, but I'd take all that she'd let me.

"One thing at a time, Si-si. It's going to be all right." I lifted her hand and pressed a kiss to the back of it. She didn't say anything more, but she squeezed my fingers in response, and settled further back against the seat.

Within five minutes, she was sound asleep.

EIGHTEEN

SIENNA

I woke to Finn carrying me again, pressed up against his warm, cedar-scented chest. At first I thought it was a dream; a memory of him hauling me out of my rapidly-sinking car. But then his arm jolted, and he cursed softly under his breath. This was no dream.

"Finn?"

"Go back to sleep, Sienna. I've got you."

"Where are we?" I blinked up at an unfamiliar ceiling.

"Hotel. Your sister's already in the next room. They only had two available since they have some people sheltering from the storm, but she insisted she didn't want to share after her *long night*."

He was sarcastic, yes, but he didn't sound angry.

"I'm sorry, Finn. She's always been selfish. I appreciate you picking her up and dealing with all of this. You're definitely on a list somewhere for sainthood, after this night. But you can put me down, now." I patted his chest.

He stopped and grinned at me, the action lopsided and showing off the miniature dimple in his right cheek. "Ready to be on your feet?"

"Yes, please."

He slowly lowered my feet to the ground, and I was pleasantly surprised to find I was no worse for the wear, besides a crick in the neck after sleeping pressed against his truck window. I rubbed it idly as I looked around the hotel room.

"So . . . that is not a very large bed."

"No, it is not. I can take the couch." He pointed to the only other furniture in the room besides the TV stand. It was barely a love seat, patterned in ancient blue floral fabric. It was so old some of the pattern had been rubbed away, leaving nothing but a shiny patch behind.

"You can't sleep on that."

"If I don't lay down in the next ten minutes, I'm going to be asleep on the floor," he drawled as he headed for the tiny bathroom. A hint of pink tile showed when he flicked on the light before stepping inside and shutting the door.

"I'll take the couch, then." I raised my voice so he could still hear me through the door.

"Don't even think about it!" he growled, surprising me.

A moment later he stepped out and washed his hands, then fixed me with a glare. "I didn't save you from a muddy riverbank to have you throw your back out before the big opening sleeping on a couch. You're taking the bed." Without waiting for further response from me, he crossed the room and dropped down onto the tiny loveseat.

The thing creaked and groaned like it was ready to give up the ghost, and I raised both eyebrows as I watched him struggle to pull off soaked leather cowboy boots. One of them popped off his foot, and he held it aloft triumphantly for a moment before dropping it to the floor with a thud. The next one followed, and a moment later he attempted to get horizontal on the couch. I watched for about ninety seconds, before walking to the door.

"This is ridiculous, Finn. It's the wee hours, and you haven't slept. I'll go next door and tell Suze she has to share with me. You take the bed, and I'll see you in a few hours, okay?" I flipped back the chain, and my hand was on the deadbolt when his fell on top of mine.

"I don't think that's a good idea. She was in a bad mood, and more than a bit tipsy."

I winced, dropping my hand from the door and letting it dangle uselessly at my side. What had I done but cause a mess, trying to clean up hers? I was useless on more than one level.

"How bad was it?"

He flattened his lips together but didn't say anything else.

"Please let me take the couch, Finn. You've done so much for us tonight, and I know you're dead on your feet. Please?" I stepped forward and slipped my arms around his sides in a half hug, leaving enough space between us that I could tip my head back and look up at him.

He ran a fingertip down the bridge of my nose, as light as a whisper over my lips, and down my chin. "Maybe we can share." The words were quiet, as if he thought I'd leap away in anger or disgust at the idea.

"I think we can make it work," I agreed without hesitation. He'd been put out more than enough on our account, no way was I denying him sleeping in a bed tonight. Besides, spending the night cuddling up next to him was an excellent night's sleep, as I recalled from our night on the couch together.

One of his eyebrows shot up in surprise, but he schooled his expression quickly. "Okay, then."

"Hopefully this time, we're far enough from home that there won't be anybody around to report the scandal to your aunt," I added drily.

He let me lead him by the hand over to the bed, and he sat on the side as I kicked off my own shoes and made a quick trip to the room's fuchsia-hued facilities. Butterflies soared in my stomach as I re-entered the bedroom and found him lying fully clothed on top of the comforter, hands laced behind his head.

I crossed to the closest side which he'd left for me, and quickly pulled myself under the blankets. Even through all of our clothes and the two layers of bedding, I could feel the warmth radiating from his side. I turned onto my side and let out a sigh.

"What is it?"

"You're like my own personal space heater. It's *glorious*."

He chuckled. "Ready for me to turn off the lamp?"

"Ready when you are."

He reached over and clicked the light off, and then it was only the two of us, alone in the dark, sharing the same air. The butterflies were still swooping around in my stomach at the proximity, but he let out a big yawn, and shifted. The motion brought him a little bit closer, and I found myself leaning to the left, hoping to catch a small snuggle.

He'd barely stopped moving before the faintest of snores escaped, and I had to hold in a giggle at how quickly he'd fallen asleep. He'd done so much for me, and not once was he accusing or angry. Worried? Yes. That had been plain as day on his handsome features. There were bags under his eyes, but still he'd followed through and taken me to get Suze in the middle of a hurricane.

He was kind, and brave, and selfless. As I scooted closer to his addictive warmth and alluring masculine scent, I felt incredibly lucky to be lying next to the man I loved, even under these circumstances. Because I did love him, even if I could only admit it in the dead of night, alone with my thoughts and the wailing wind outside. One day, I hoped to be brave enough to tell him.

Nineteen

Repercussions

Sienna

The next day dawned with tepid light from the window, and a sinking feeling of all we'd have to deal with. For starters, the two-hour drive home with Suze. After that, I already knew the power was out at home, and I needed to go check on the shop and make sure it had fared well. At least there wasn't a fridge full of food there, already starting to spoil. *Ugh.* I wanted nothing more than to roll over, snuggle up against Finn's back, and pretend-sleep the morning away. Unfortunately, his side was empty and had already gone cold.

A rude knock at the door shook me the rest of the way out of my denial.

"Sienna, are you in there? I'm starving, and I'm out of cash. Can you slip me a five under the door? Better make it ten. There's surely a breakfast burrito in this town somewhere," she groused.

I lay flat on my back, staring up at the water-stained ceiling as I counted to ten before rolling out of bed and crossing to open the door. I forgot about the chain, so when I tried to open it, it snapped back against the door frame and nearly caught my thumb in the process. I snatched it back in the nick of time and reached up to flick the chain off the door.

When it swung open, Suze's gaze skidded over me as she let out a low whistle. When I turned, I saw why. My startled yelp had drawn Finn from the bathroom, wrapped in nothing but a towel. He was damp from the shower, and I had to forcibly avert my eyes from his nicely-muscled chest. Suze wasn't so polite, and a flood of jealousy swamped me at the way she was ogling him.

"Hey!" I snapped my fingers to get her attention back to my face. "We all need breakfast. Give us a couple of minutes to get dressed, and we'll get something together."

"Mmm, I don't know. Not really interested in being the third wheel in this little morning-after breakfast." She whirled her finger around between me and

Finn, who retreated into the bathroom to avoid her roving gaze.

"If you mean the morning after I almost got caught in a flood trying to rescue your sorry rear end, then yes, it *is* the morning after that. Thanks for noticing," I said drily. "I need ten minutes." Without waiting for a response, I shut the door, and headed for the sink to splash some water on my face and clean up the best I could.

Twenty minutes later we'd checked out and hit a drive-through for breakfast. We all munched quietly in the car, still tired from the stressful night. A car insurance adjuster had called. My car had indeed flooded and was being totaled as a result. Frankly, I was trying not to think about how much I didn't have time to deal with that.

"So, are you two a *real* item now?" Suze asked from the back seat of the truck.

"Yes," we both said at the same time. I shot Finn a smile, amused by our adamant agreement.

"Huh. So, the town crazy actually did something for once. I didn't see that coming. Interesting."

I turned in my seat to face her. "So, since we're talking relationships, where is Mister 'Something came up,' who had you bail on your job?"

She rolled her eyes and sighed. "We're over. It was fun while it lasted, but in the end we wanted different things." She shrugged noncommittally, and to my endless irritation didn't even *mention* the trouble she'd caused at work.

"Uh-huh. And what was that?"

"I wanted adventure, he ran home to his ex. It happens. So, do you think I can get my job back, now that I'm home and you're the office hero?"

I was wrong. It was *worse* when she asked about work.

"Absolutely not. I got raked over the coals for *your* irresponsibility." I turned around and slammed my back against the seat, trying to hold in the bitter words that wanted to fly out at her flippancy. I took a deep breath and forced it out my nose angrily.

"Ooh, she's mad now. Finn, did she do the bull nose thing in high school? Do you remember? Because I don't remember when it started, but if she does that, you know she's good and ticked."

I closed my eyes, trying to maintain at least the appearance of calm. This was what Suze did; she blew something apart for the sheer fun of it, and then antagonized *you* for being upset at her path of destruction.

"Uhm, not that I remember? I can't say I recall her ever being that angry with me," Finn murmured, looking at me out of the corner of his eyes.

Suze was quiet for a moment, then muttered, "That's because she saves all her anger for *me*. My own twin, and she likes everybody else better than me."

That did it. I snapped and hung around the back of the seat to glare at her. "Are you *serious* right now? I like everybody else better than you? Forgive me, Suze, for being human. I love you, but the way you do whatever you want and leave everybody else to clean up your mess is not endearing! Do you know how much trouble you've caused? Not even at work, though you caused plenty there, too. I got my car stuck by a river last night and it flooded. Completely. The insurance is totaling it, and my shop opens in barely a week! How am I supposed to get to work Monday? Hmm? And to my new business, after that? But you don't think about anyone else, do you? It's all Suze, all the time. Maybe I'd like you more if we spent time together having fun, instead of you leaving me behind to clean up your mess *constantly*."

"Wow," she said, her mouth making a large, exaggerated O. "You've been sitting on that a while, huh? Let it out, baby sister. I can take it."

"Oh. My. Freaking—" I bit my tongue and turned back around. It wasn't worth it. She was immune to censure, even that which she wholeheartedly deserved. I took two more deep breaths, and didn't bother to look at her when I said, "Suze, this is it. The last time. I put myself and Finn in danger last night to help you, and you can't even be serious about the consequences. The next time you run off, you can get yourself home. I'm *done.*"

Finn reached over and squeezed my fingers, conveying his silent support.

"Fine, Sienna. Fine. I get it, I ruined your perfect little fairytale life. I get it, I'm the screwup. Well, I hope you enjoy being the perfect one all the time. Tell me when we're back in town; I'm putting on my headphones." She rustled around in her purse, and then the backseat fell silent.

I was too busy sitting rigid as a board, staring straight ahead and gripping Finn's knuckles like my own personal lifeline to respond. Even my own life being put in danger didn't faze her.

She could get mad and say whatever she wanted, but I meant it; I was done wrecking my own life for her. I had dreams, a wonderful man in my life, and hard work ahead of me. I wasn't giving that up to chase Suze down ever again.

"You okay?" Finn asked quietly, presumably to not be heard through Suze's headphones.

"Not really, but thanks for asking." I gave him a tight smile. It wasn't his fault, or his problem to fix.

"I'm here if you'd like to talk about all this later . . . For what it's worth, I'm glad you're safe. We can figure out the car, but you're irreplaceable. And you were brave to go after your sister. Even if she isn't able to say it, I am sure she appreciates it. You didn't see her last night, but she was soaked to the bone, huddled outside a dark truck stop completely alone when we pulled up and got her. She has to know what a bad situation that was."

I closed my eyes and nodded, easily able to picture the scene he'd painted. And still, my sister couldn't be a normal, grateful human being about it. "She's always been defensive, Finn. It's just . . . it's our lives, at this point. Thank you for coming, and for driving us home."

"I'll always come for you, Sienna. You mean the world to me. When I saw your car, and the water rising last night, it was like everything moved in slow motion. I couldn't see anything except you getting swept away, and it clarified a lot of things for me." He gave my fingers a small squeeze. "It's absolutely the worst time to ever say it, given our company"—he nodded over his shoulder towards Suze—"but I don't want to wait anymore. I love you, Sienna. I know we haven't been together long, but the thought of losing you last night made me crazy. I won't freak you out with *commitment* stuff, but . . . I'm all in. You and me, we're a package deal from now on."

Tears welled up in my eyes at his words, and I leaned over the middle console to rest my forehead on his bicep. I clutched his hand in both of mine and planted small kisses on his arm. I whispered the words, too chicken to say them loudly, but he heard all the same.

"I love you too, Finn. I love you too." *And it scared me to death.*

As soon as we made it inside the Adele city limits, Suze's headphones disappeared, and she asked to be dropped off at Jude's diner. Finn swung that way, and he'd barely stopped the truck in the parking lot before she dove out without a backwards look, sashaying across the parking lot and into the building.

Finn shook his head at her hasty retreat, but I stared straight ahead. "Do you want to go home, or somewhere else?" he asked as he steered us back onto the road.

"Do you mind if we swing by the shop? My power was out when I left last night, so I'm sure I've got cleanup to do there. If we do a quick walkthrough of the shop I can focus on the house."

"Absolutely."

We drove those five minutes in silence, still tired from so little sleep. I was looking out the window, mind wandering about what colors I'd have to get to make post-hurricane sky-blue when Finn sucked in a breath. I jerked my head around to see what it was, and nearly cried. Where the shop used to be, the branches of the large oak in the middle of the parking lot were all we could see. Its roots dangled limply in the air, and, in the time it took us to pick around the parking lot and find a clear space to park, I said a hundred silent prayers that the shop had been miraculously spared on the other side of all that mess.

"Finn, what if it's ruined? I'm supposed to open in a week." My hands knotted together in my lap, knuckles white from the strain of holding it together.

"Hey, look at me," he urged as he put the truck in park. "Whatever we find in there, it's going to be okay. We *will* make this work. If there's damage, hopefully it's minimal. Trees come down all the time, and it's dealt with. We'll do the same." I quickly glanced at him to nod, before riveting my eyes back on the mass of limbs blocking us from seeing the front of the shop.

My knees felt numb when I climbed down from his truck, and somewhere in my brain it registered that I was still in my pajamas, in the middle of the town. I didn't care, just hurried across the debris-littered lot to go around the ancient downed tree. What I saw made my stomach sink all the way down to my feet. The front of the shop was engulfed by the top of the tree, and there was no way to access the shop.

Finn stopped a step behind me, letting me absorb what this meant without interference. I stood there for an agonizing moment before going around to the back entrance. My fingers didn't want to work as I pulled the key out of my pocket. I fumbled and dropped them and tried again with more care. The lock clicked open with a hint of finality, and my shoulders were tight as I pushed the door inward. The first step inside, my heart sank as my shoe squelched on the wet floor.

"Careful, the floor is wet," I said quietly. Finn rested his hand on my shoulder and rubbed it for a second before letting go so I could lead the way in. The damage got worse the farther in we walked.

The large panes of glass which made up the storefront had shattered to glitter on the floor, scattered across the entire front room from the force. Tree limbs obscured the front, jabbing in through the roof as well as the windows. Hunks of wet ceiling material littered the floor and slumped over the top of my brand-new shelving units, and I had to choke back a sob at the destruction in the beautiful gallery. The largest limb had landed there, and most of the art we'd already hung was down.

I stopped in the arched doorway, covering my mouth with my hand to muffle the sobs that had broken free. Finn tucked me under his arm and whispered soothing words.

"It's going to be okay, Sienna. It's going to be okay."

"Finn, this is it. The shop is destroyed, the art is destroyed." I gestured to the downed paintings, the water and debris on the ground, and then back towards the store shelving. "This . . . this is it. We aren't opening next week. I need to call Greg. He needs to call the insurance company. I guess I do, too, for that matter," I added, thinking of my renter's insurance. It would cover what I'd spent on supplies at least. But it wouldn't bring my beautiful little shop

back, or the art pieces people had entrusted me w
ith.

I sunk my head into my hands, and then scrubbed listlessly at my tear-soaked cheeks. Crying wouldn't help anything, but I couldn't seem to stop, regardless. My heart was broken, littered on the ground amidst the rubble which was all that remained of my dream.

I walked over to the back wall, where a single painting still hung without a scratch. It was my charcoal drawing of the bench, and I ran my finger over it sadly. It was a rain-soaked reminder of all that couldn't be.

"I'll call him," Finn agreed grimly.

"Thank you," I said, dropping my fingers, and turning my back on the gallery room, and the dream it had held so beautifully.

TWENTY

Labor Day

SIENNA

T he next few days were some of the worst in my life. A company came out and removed the tree that had smashed the shop, but the damage remained. Greg the landlord was great, but he warned me that insurance was never fast, and hurricanes made it worse. It would likely be months before they cut the check to repair the shop, and *then* the work had to be done.

He managed a crew to cover the roof and bring in fans and dehumidifiers to start removing the water, while Finn and I tried to pull out as many of the supplies as were salvageable. By Sunday night, I was exhausted, had blisters on my hands from all the heavy lifting, and emotionally wrung out. I felt like an animated shell of the person I was before the storm had blown through.

We'd lost nearly half of the shop's inventory. The shelving would survive, though ironically I had nowhere to store all of it. Finn had promised to secure a spot with a friend. Thankfully all but two pieces of the gallery art had been salvageable, and I was going to coordinate their return over the next few weeks. Everyone had been gracious, and the two who'd been destroyed had agreed that I could itemize them as part of the insurance claim, so at least they'd be paid. My heart hurt on so many levels, though, that it didn't feel like a resolution.

My mom picked me up bright and early Monday morning to drive me to work since I didn't have my rental car yet. She had a compassionate smile, but I felt dead inside as she drove the familiar route to my office. She chattered about all the storm damage, but I mostly zoned out and stared at the road slipping by outside my window. Her words finally broke through the fog as she pulled up to the front door of the building. The new secretary sat at her desk, where Suze had so briefly worked.

". . . I know it's sad, but really, you've got a good job here. Starting a small shop was so risky. Frankly I'm glad you're staying put. This job has benefits, and those are hard to come by. Maybe this has worked out for the best. You'll see in time." She patted me on the arm, and I had to resist the urge to yank it away. She'd never understood, but her callous words felt like a slap in the face after the weekend I'd had.

"Thanks for the ride, Mom," I murmured and climbed out, not responding to her opinion on my shattered dreams. It was done anyway, so it wasn't worth fighting over anymore.

I badged in, waved blandly to the new secretary—she was so enthusiastic, the complete opposite of my mood today—and was settling down in my cubicle when a text came through from Finn.

Finn: Have a good day at work. I'm going to finish the cleanup with Greg, so you can take the rest of the week off. We'll reconvene Saturday night?

Saturday night. The night we were supposed to have the inaugural gallery. My heart was so pulverized at this point that I didn't think it could hurt more, but it stung afresh at the reminder.

Sienna: Thank you, Finn.

I probably should have said more, but I was too numb to try. Finn had been a rock through the whole experience, while I'd fallen apart.

I hadn't expected it to hit me this hard, but to be so close to something I never dreamed I could have and then for it to be ripped away? It was unbearable.

I turned the phone on silent and tucked it in my drawer. I needed some space to grieve, and I hoped he'd understand.

I worked the rest of the day in numb oblivion, picked up my rental car, and went to bed early. The next few days were more of the same, interspersed with texts from Finn. He'd reached out doggedly, despite my less-than-enthusiastic replies. He was too good to be treated that way, but I was like a zombie, walking in a fog each day and going through the motions.

Tamika noticed, too, and called me on it Wednesday.

"Girl, you've got to snap out of this. You lost your shop, yes. But your life still has hope. You've got a hottie beating your door down—don't push him away too. Don't let one bad thing spiral into more," she chided gently when I ignored one of his texts while we were in the breakroom.

"I know, Tamika, and I will. I don't know how to pretend to be happy right now. I'm not. I'm miserable, and it doesn't feel fair to take it out on him when he's put in at least as much effort as I have.

I need some time to recover, and then we'll go back to normal."

"Sienna, a man like that wants to work through it *with* you. He's a keeper, and you're pushing him away like he's one of Suze's distraction men. He's the real thing, and this is not how you deal with this. I love you, girl, and it kills me to see you like this."

"Tamika, I appreciate where you're coming from, but I have to work through this. If he really loves me, he'll wait. It's not perfect, but it's where I'm at right now." I wasn't angry with her, but I didn't have any energy left inside me to argue the point further, even with one of my besties. I turned around and walked out of the breakroom without waiting on the sub-par coffee to be ready.

Friday found me still wooden, answering client emails for the nearly finished Confectionary Delights project. It was tedious, but they'd asked for one last small adjustment. I assigned it to Bryan. If I tried to do it right now, I'd probably turn all the festive watercolors black, and they'd fire me. Wouldn't that be the coup de grâce?

Bryan responded back that he'd have the changes done by two o'clock, and I leaned back in my desk chair to stare up at the ceiling.

My phone rang, and without checking I lifted it to my ear.

"Hello?"

"Sienna! I'm so glad I caught you. I know you're at work, but I've been worried and there's a lot to tell you about the shop—"

"Finn, I—I'm sorry. I know I haven't answered, but . . . can we leave it for tomorrow? I don't have it in me today."

"Okay, tomorrow. But it can't wait past tomorrow, okay?"

"Okay."

"I love you, Sienna. It's all going to work out, I promise." He said it resolutely, and I wished in that moment I had a tenth of the faith he had.

"I love you too, Finn. See you tomorrow."

I clicked off the phone and continued staring at the ceiling. Barely a moment later, it rang again.

"I've got to put this on vibrate," I muttered as I held it back to my ear. "Hello?"

A low wail was the first thing I heard, and I sat bolt upright in my desk chair. "Hello? What's going on?"

"Sienna!" Jenny's breathless tone broke through the background noise. "Marlie's in labor, and it's all hands on deck. She wants you at the hospital; can you come?"

I jumped out of my chair, my pulse suddenly frantic as I threw random stuff in my purse. "Of course, Jenny, I'm at work but tell her I'm on the way. Shoot, I've got to tell my boss. Be there so soon. Does she need anything?"

"Yes, FOOD!" Marlie hollered over the receiver, which must have been on speaker.

"Ignore her. She's not allowed to eat. She's mad because the nurse just told her so."

I chuckled for the first time in a week as I hung up the phone and looked down at my purse. I'd thrown in the stapler in my hurry, so I dug that back out, and jogged across the floor to where Barbara sat, serenely typing some memo or another for Randy.

"Barbara! Can you please tell Randy I've got to leave early? My friend is in labor, and she needs me at the hospital." I'd already taken two steps away before she responded.

"Wait, Sienna! This was for you." She gestured at the email she'd been typing up. "He'd like to see you for a moment in his office. I'm glad we caught you before you left," she said with a motherly smile.

I tried to hide my grimace as she slowly rose and knocked on his office door and told him I was here. She waved me in, and I tried not to look as impatient as I felt when I perched on the edge of the chair across from his desk.

Randy was leaned back in his executive's chair, hands steepled thoughtfully over his chest. "So, Sienna, I hear you've got an urgent situation, so I'll make this quick."

Yes please. I nodded and forced a small smile. It was probably a grimace, but who was counting?

"I'd like to offer you the assistant art director position. The partners and I have been mulling it for a while, but you've really risen above the rest with this Confectionary Delights project."

My jaw dropped at the unexpected news. My brain skipped about twelve beats before I asked, "What about Bryan? I'm sure you know he's expecting that position." *And I'd never hear the end of it if I got it instead.*

"If you accept, we'll speak with him. I know he's hungry to advance, but you've got a raw talent we can't ignore, and the leadership skills to back it up. You're well-liked here, Sienna, and we appreciate your hard work."

"Wow . . . thank you. I don't even know what to say," I stammered.

"Well, I was hoping you'd say yes. But, take the weekend to think about it, and I'll expect to hear your answer Monday. Sound fair?"

I nodded, too flabbergasted for much else. They were choosing me over Bryan? Truly?

"All right, then. Don't you need to get going?" He raised his eyebrows.

"Oh! Yes! Marlie's having her baby."

He chuckled as I leapt out of the chair and left his office in a rush.

"Drive safely, dear!" Barbara called to my retreating back. I waved over my shoulder as I rushed out the front door.

The hospital smelled like astringent, making me wrinkle my nose as I came out of the elevator on the labor & delivery floor. It was all shiny white as far as the eye could see, aside from the pink and blue hats lining the walls at fun angles as if they were dancing along. I pressed a button for admittance, and gave my name to the nurse who buzzed me in.

Each room I passed was a festival of noises, until I arrived at Marlie's, where another low moan rolled out as I knocked softly.

"Come in!" Jenny called, so I pushed my way in and shut it quietly behind me. Marlie was sitting on a giant ball wearing a hospital gown, her eyes closed and Tucker rubbing her shoulders from his position standing behind her.

"How's it going in here?"

"Crazy. She won't take the drugs," Jenny muttered, shooting a significant glance over to where Marlie and Tucker were swaying.

Marlie moaned again, low in her throat, and Tucker helped her to her feet. She turned to face him, wrapping her arms around his neck for support as a contraction wracked her body. We stood silent, waiting for it to pass.

When it did, they stilled, her head resting on his chest. He whispered words of encouragement in her ear and pushed sweaty strands of hair from her face; a knot rose in my throat at the sight.

"They're so good together, aren't they?" Jenny whispered.

"They're perfect. Can I do anything?"

She shrugged. "Birthing is a lot of waiting. She's close, though. We could probably use some more ice, but I'll go get it." She scooped up the ugly mauve pitcher and trotted out of the room.

"I'm glad you're here," Marlie said, settling back onto her ball. "I love Jenny, but she needs someone to elbow her when it's time to hush."

"Ahh, I see. Luckily for you, I have very pointy elbows, and I'm not afraid to use them." I assumed my best elbowing stance, and jokingly batted them back and forth to demonstrate.

She laughed and then groaned, leaning back against Tucker.

"Honey, something's different. I—I think it might be time."

"Time?" he repeated, bewildered.

"For the nurse—ohhhh . . ." She drew the sound out on a lingering exhale. "I think the baby is ready."

"Oh, *time!*" He started to step away, but she locked her fingers around the sleeves of his shirt and held on like he was a wild bull.

"You stay, I'll get the nurse!" I volunteered and hurried out the door. "Excuse me, we need the nurse for room two-twenty-five. She thinks it's time to push."

A blonde nurse with gray-streaked hair leapt out of her chair and followed hot on my heels back into the room. She snapped on a fresh pair of gloves and was all business. I watched on tenterhooks as she directed Marlie back to the bed, checked her, and pronounced that it was indeed time to push.

Jenny came back in, and the two of us were shuffled to the side of the room as everything began to happen at once. Marlie panted on the bed, gazing into Tucker's eyes like he was the only thing holding her to the earth, while a stream of nurses, doctors, and staff streamed in and out with all of the delivery equipment. I perched on the edge of the tiny couch, holding my breath as everyone moved in a choreographed dance in scrubs.

Within a few moments, everything calmed, and everyone streamed back out except the doctor and two nurses. Jenny was called forward to Marlie's other side, and me to her head. I held a cool rag on her brow as she pushed. Once, twice, three times—and her little man slid free and began to wail in the doctor's hands.

"It's a boy, and he's got healthy lungs!" We all cheered as she set the baby onto Marlie's chest. I stepped back as Tucker leaned in and kissed Marlie. I heard him murmur softly to her that she'd done so well, and he was so proud of her. In that tender moment, something that I didn't know had been frozen in my heart melted free. *That* was true, unconditional love, and I was honored to stand witness to it. A tear rolled down my cheek, and I hurriedly dashed it away with the heel of my hand.

We all took turns admiring little Shane, and then Jenny and I left to let Marlie get her rest. I was surprised to find it was dark when I walked to my car, so absorbed had I been in the birth and everything after. I was exhausted, but my heart was full.

TWENTY-ONE

The Big Reveal

SIENNA

S aturday morning, I woke to a text from Finn. I was still riding an emotional high from the night before, and in a better mood than I'd been since before the storm. Something about the beauty of new life *clarified* things. I rubbed my bleary eyes and read his message with a smile.

Finn: Hey Si-si, I'm sure it was a late night, but I'd love to do lunch with you. I'll pick it up and bring it if you're willing to meet me at the shop?

I sighed, running my hands through my hair, fanning it idly out over my pillow. I was past ready to see him, after my self-imposed week of isolation. But the shop was going to depress me again. Seeing it all empty and broken, after all the love we'd poured into it.

I was a big girl, though, and after taking my time to grieve, I had to come to grips. Finn would help me, if I let him.

Sienna: Absolutely. Noon? I've missed you this week. Sorry for everything.

Finn: Sorry for what?

I bit my lip, trying to find the words to say what didn't want to be said.

Sienna: I'm sorry for retreating. Leaving you to handle the mess. That stops today. I'll see you at noon. XOXO

Finn: No apologies necessary. I've missed you too. XOXO

I got ready with a smile and put in the extra time to make myself look nice since it had been a whole week. I had a lot of making up to do, and while he would never complain if I showed up in a baggy t-shirt and paint-covered sweats, it felt nice to dress up again. I picked out a fun sun dress and sensible flats, did my makeup, and stared in the mirror at my hair. My purple roots had long since grown out—I'd been too busy to make my usual trip to the salon—so I pulled it into a fancy Dutch braid, and promised myself I'd make a salon appointment for Monday evening.

Monday, the day my boss wanted an answer on the new job. I needed to talk about that with Finn, too. I donned my dress and shoes and walked to the corner of my living room where my easel was set to catch the sunlight. I hadn't touched it in a week, and the painting on it was nearly finished. I hadn't had anything in mind for it when I began, I'd only wanted to capture the moment that was burned so vividly in my brain.

It was yet another thing I promised myself I'd get back to this week. And I would. I had a plan for it now, sparkling as brightly as the morning sun through my window. I checked the clock and threw on an apron so I could do a bit of work on it before I went to meet Finn. It was time for my life to move forward, and I was finally ready.

Noon found me leaning against the hood of my car in the shop's parking lot, with my head tilted back to bask in the sunshine. The tree had been removed, nothing to show where it had fallen but a fine layer of sawdust and the brown tarp on the shop's roof. Finn's truck pulled in a moment later, and I straightened, eager to see him after a miserable week. Why had I waited an entire week? Now that he was so close, all I wanted was to fling myself into his arms, and burrow into his solid, comforting chest for a hug

.

He parked on the other side of my car and stepped out of the truck juggling takeout bags from Jude's and Sweet Nothings. He pushed the door shut with his foot, and then turned to grin at me.

"I'm so glad to see you," he said before setting everything down on the hood of my rental and crossing to stand in front of me. He hesitated for a brief second, and then stepped forward and opened his arms wide. I leaned into him, the hug better even than my best memory, and tension I didn't know I'd been holding in my shoulders drained away like dirty dishwater from a sink.

We clung to each other for a few minutes, neither of us willing to separate now that we were back together. Eventually I leaned back, looking up at his perfectly handsome face. His glasses were smudged, like he'd been working and shoved them up his nose, and the small imperfection made me love him more.

"I've missed you so much. I'm sorry I pulled back. I was hurting, and I didn't know how to process that any other way. It probably makes me the worst girlfriend in the history of forever, but—"

He planted a kiss on my lips to cut me off, and then shook his head. "You needed some time, and you don't have to apologize for it. Do I wish I could have done more for you? Absolutely. I would love to be the one to take all of your pain if I could. But I'm not angry. I do have something to show you, though, before we start on lunch. Are you ready?" He nodded over to the new front door on the shop. I'd noticed they'd put up a new door, and that the front windows were covered, but I hadn't wandered closer yet.

I forced a smile and nodded. "Whenever you are."

Finn took me by the hand and led me to the front door. I looked down at my toes as he unlocked it and pushed it open for us. Steeling myself for the empty pit of the inside, I looked up.

Confusion, followed by awe, washed over me.

"What in the— How? Finn, this place was completely trashed. I don't understand; how does it look this good? I thought you were cleaning it out this week, but everything's back in place. The ceiling's even there. It was ruined. I, I—" I gripped his forearm tightly, scared to blink lest the beautiful, once-again-clean, polished, and stocked store in front of me vanish before my eyes.

"It was simple enough, really. I got together with Greg, and explained how important this was to you, and that we didn't want to wait months to get the art shop open. He spoke with the insurance company, and they agreed that due to the storm we could extensively photograph and then begin repairs. So, we did. You and I did a lot of the cleanup, and Greg called in a crew first thing Monday to get the debris out, so I had a clean slate. I called in a few more favors with the Fergusons, George pitched in . . . they did a lot, really. Then I did my best to remember exactly how it was and put it back." He shrugged one shoulder, as if he hadn't performed a miracle in the span of five days.

"The roof will still have to be replaced, but Greg promised that it would be scheduled, and you'd be notified in advance, so it won't mess up any events you might need to hold. That part could take a bit, what with the hurricane damage being so heavy in the area." We both stood frozen in the doorway, as I looked and looked, small details jumping out at me everywhere of things he'd carefully returned to their former glory.

"Finn, if you'd told me last week you'd do this, I would have thought you were crazy, that it was too much to do in a month, let alone five days. This is so incredible. I think I'm going to cry again." I sniffed, desperately wanting to hold back the tears.

"Happy tears?"

"Ecstatic, awed, amazed tears," I corrected, and squeezed his fingers tightly before letting go to explore the rest of the building. He followed me from room to room, silently letting me take it all in. The classroom had been untouched besides the water which ran in, so it looked the same as we'd left it.

My point-of-sale system in the back had been replaced with a new model, since the old one was damaged by the water. The last room I headed for was the gallery. It had taken the worst damage, and I was sure that he hadn't been able to put it back. There was no way, since the original had taken us so long to get right.

And yet, when I walked in, the soft aqua walls glowed in the light of a new chandelier, twinkling softly overhead. The big front windows had been replaced and covered with brown paper while the construction was ongoing. The only difference was that where the art previously hung, there were now empty spaces, save one.

I walked over and stood before it, looking up at Finn's favorite piece of the bench on a rainy afternoon. I reverently lifted a finger, brushing over the surface.

"It was the only thing in here that survived exactly how it was, and I took that as a sign that it needed to stay," he said, wrapping me up in a hug from behind. I leaned back against Finn's chest and closed my eyes.

"You thought of every detail. I'm just . . . amazed. How did you do all of this, and still go to work?" I looked up over my shoulder at him, taking in his five o'clock shadow, and the bags under his eyes.

"I didn't. I called in, took the week off, and fixed it. I wasn't sure it would be done by today, but everyone really came out and helped. You'd be amazed, Sienna, how many people want to see this place open."

I spun in his arms, cupping his face with my hands, and rubbing my thumbs slowly over his cheeks. "Finn, you're incredible." I peppered his face with little teasing kisses as I said, "Thank you, thank you, thank you. This is the absolute opposite of what I expected. I was planning to walk through an empty, destroyed shell and try not to cry. Now, I'm crying for a completely different reason. This is the best gift." I shook my head, more words refusing to come out around the lump in my throat.

He smiled lazily, showing off that tiny dimple in his cheek, and leaned in to kiss me. It was quick, a playful peck that left me wanting more. I tried to follow him, but he held up a finger, stopping me.

"There's one more thing. Come on." He nodded to the end of the gallery, and I followed him, curious. What else could there be? He'd shown me the whole shop.

At the end of the gallery, he paused at the end of a drop cloth. "Are you ready?"

"Uhm, yes?"

His eyes gleamed as he pulled back the cover. Underneath was a tidy stack of art pieces, cleaned up and ready to hang.

"I spoke to some of the locals who contributed art to the gallery and told them what I was trying to do. Two of them came in throughout the week, and got each and every piece ready to hang, except the two which were destroyed. One had a second piece to submit, and there's one space left. If you have something in mind, you can fill it. Aunt Dolly has been on a mission for the last twenty-four hours, calling all of the local papers, putting up bulletins at the church here and in all three surrounding counties, contacting art schools . . . I don't even know how many people she's called. Once she gets on a mission, she's unstoppable. All I know is, she told me to expect a crowd."

"A crowd . . ."

"Tonight. Si-si, the show is still on. We've got paintings to hang after we finish lunch." Finn watched intently, waiting for it to click. When it did, I nearly flew out of my skin.

"You put my show back together? And the show is happening *tonight*?"

"It's happening tonight." He nodded, and at that, I flung myself into his arms so hard, I nearly bowled him off his feet. This time, the kiss was long and slow, and I felt it down to the tips of my toes. When we pulled apart, he had a slightly dazed expression on his face.

"That was incredible. We should have hurricanes more often," he joked.

"Bite your *tongue* and let's get these paintings on the wall!" I lightly punched his arm, and he laughed, and pulled out his tools.

We had work to do.

Twenty-Two

Not Yo' Mama's Man

Sienna

The afternoon passed in a blink, between hanging paintings and going home to change into more appropriate attire for the art expo. I put on a simple black slip dress, my most sparkly heels, and a teardrop necklace to tie it together.

Finn was meeting me at the shop, and as I pulled into the employee parking lot in the back, my nerves danced the samba. This was it. My dream, pulled back from the brink of death by Finn, the man of my dreams who I hadn't even known I was looking for.

I slipped in the back door and was surprised to find Bea and Celia from the bakery in pink catering uniforms, fussing over a delectable table of miniature sweets.

"Hey, congratulations!" Bea crossed over and gave me a quick hug. "Are you excited for the big night?"

"Hi, yes. Excited, and nervous," I admitted, smoothing down the front of my dress for the tenth time since I'd put it on an hour ago.

"Well, you look stunning, and so does your new place." Celia leaned over and gave me a quick hug and a peck on the cheek. "Don't worry about us, we've got some more things to bring in from the delivery van, but we'll stay out of your hair. I'm sure you've got some last-minute arranging to do." Her eyes crinkled at the corners, the familiar smile lines framing them perfectly.

"I'm sure there's something," I agreed, and walked on through the shop. We'd added twinkle lights to the tops of each of the freestanding shelves for ambiance earlier and dimmed the overhead lighting to give the space an elegant warmth, and the effect left light pouring from the gallery, like a perfect invitation to wander in and enjoy the display. I walked in, and started at the beginning, circling the room piece by piece, tweaking anything that needed it.

On the last piece, Finn walked in. He was wearing a tuxedo, and my mouth went dry at the sight of him.

His hair was freshly trimmed and slicked back, the earlier stubble shaved clean, and a black tie holding his snow-white shirt closed at his throat. My eyes traced up to meet his, taking in the whole, undeniably gorgeous package that was Finn. And he was every bit as gorgeous on the inside, which was why I loved him with my whole heart.

He crossed the few steps between us, and I held out my hand for his. Our palms slid together, and our fingers entwined as if we'd been a couple forever, not a few short months. And truly, he felt like forever. The thought surprised me, but for the first time in my life, it didn't terrify me.

"You look magnificent this evening," he said, his voice a low rumble that made heat bloom in my belly.

"So do you. Truly, you're a work of art yourself."

One corner of his lips quirked up in a soft smile. "Good thing I'm standing in a gallery."

I snorted at his silly joke, shaking my head. He never ceased to make me laugh, and I loved that about him.

"Come on, I have something to show *you* for once." I tugged him across the gallery, to the center space I'd asked him to leave empty for one more piece earlier. A sheet hung over it now, maintaining the mystery.

"The final piece. Is it one of yours?"

I nodded, suddenly anxious at the idea of him seeing it. What if he hated it?

"Do I get to see it early?"

"Yes, you do. Close your eyes."

He obeyed, and I slipped my fingers free to carefully remove the sheet, folding it up and tucking it under my arm. "Okay, open." I held my breath as his warm brown eyes opened, and he drank in the painting I'd made.

"It's me," he said softly, stepping forward as if to touch it.

"It is. Do you like it?" I asked, a quaver sneaking into the question. I tried to see it with fresh perspective, the colors rioting on the canvas, but working together at the same time. The splash of cerulean on his shirt collar, the deep brown umber I'd mixed especially for his eyes. It was a cacophony and a symphony on paper. But every line and every stroke was *Finn*.

"It's . . . stunning. Do I really look this good?" he joked, looking over to where I stood, hands tucked under my arms.

"You look better. I'm not sure I did you justice. But that day at the auction, something about your smile, and the way your glasses framed your eyes . . . I had to capture that moment, that feeling. I wanted to keep it always, even if things didn't work out between us."

The smile he shot my way at that nearly turned my knees to jelly. "Well, you achieved it. Are you going to sell me to some wealthy buyer tonight?" he asked, looking scandalized at the thought.

I chuckled. "Not this one, no. This one is for you, if you'd like to have it."

"I love it, but I'd need one of you to go next to it. Can I commission one of you, in the same style?"

"Hmm, I don't know." I rubbed my chin, pretending to think it over. "You *can* have whatever you want."

He placed his hands on my bare shoulders, the simple touch sending goosebumps down my arms. "I've got everything I want, right here in front of me."

"So do I. Remember before, when I said I was afraid of commitment and—" I swallowed hard, wondering if I really wanted to say what I was about to say. I did. "Of marriage?"

He nodded solemnly.

"I think I was wrong. You've become so important to me, Finn. In ways I didn't know were possible, and you've made me feel loved and supported, and like the most important person in your world."

"You *are* the most important person in my world," he murmured, searching my eyes to see where I was going with this.

I forced myself to keep going. "I think that the reason I was scared before, is because I'd never found the right person. My parents? They weren't right. I can see that now, looking back. But what I feel for you is different. You and I—we're meant to be. You've *never* left me or let me down, even when that would have been the rational thing to do. And it's starting to feel . . . like forever." I shrugged one shoulder lightly, not sure what else to say. He was so good, and steady, and I knew without an ounce of doubt that he wasn't going to abandon me like my father had.

Finn smiled and pulled me back to his chest for a hug. When he rested his chin on the top of my head, I snuggled in closer—thoughts of wrinkling my dress long forgotten—I melted into him, and he into me. "Sienna, I'm glad to hear you feel that way. Because I feel the same. The day you saved my bacon on that auction block, I had hope. Hope for more; hope for the future. Then, we went on a mind-blowing first date. And I was drawn even further to you. Your drive, your passion. You're so full of life, like no one else I've ever met. Since the moment of our first kiss, I've known that you were the one for me. My future, my love, my soul mate." He pulled back from the hug and ran a hand through his hair. Was it shaking? Why was he shaking?

"I hadn't intended to do this yet, because I didn't want to scare you, or push you away. But it feels right. So, I'm going to go for it."

"Go for what, Finn? You've already done everything, what else is there to go for?" I gestured at the gorgeous room we stood in, the culmination of all his hard work and sheer determination.

He reached into his tuxedo pocket and pulled out a little black velvet box before sinking to one knee, right there on the gallery floor. My hands flew to my mouth of their own accord, and tears prickled the back of my eyes as the man of my dreams began to speak.

"Sienna Leigh Thompson, you light up my life. You bring color to a world that was gray, and even my worst days aren't so bad because you're in them. I promise to love you every single minute of forever, if you would do me the honor of becoming my wife."

His eyes shone as he added one more thing. "Whenever *you're* ready. We can have as long of an engagement as you'd like."

I reached down, and pulled him up off the floor, tears threatening to spill as I spoke. "Finn Russell,

I would marry you at the courthouse tonight if I could. Yes, I will be your wife."

He scooped me up, crushing the ring box between us as he swung me around in a circle, and I heard applause from the end of the gallery. He set me down, and we both turned to see a small crowd gathered, his aunt at the front in glittering evening attire.

"Finny, you're like a son to me and I am so terribly proud of you, but if you get married at a courthouse I will disown you. We will plan a wedding and invite the whole town, exactly how it should be." She sniffed and pulled a tissue from her sleeve before dabbing her nose with it delicately.

He looked over at me and raised an eyebrow, as if to see what I thought about her statement.

I grinned, and said, "I guess we'll have to have the whole town, then. Do you think Aunt Dolly will plan it for us?"

"I accept!" she called, and a mix of cheers and laughter went up from the crowd of patrons gathered behind her.

With a grin, Finn slipped the ring on my hand, and pressed another slow, lingering kiss to my lips. When he pulled back, I was breathless, but so, so happy.

"Ready to welcome your guests for the evening?" Finn asked, shooting a glance at the growing crowd lingering in the doorway.

"It seems like we should. You *did* go to all the trouble to save my expo, after all." I squeezed both of his hands, excitement flowing through me like rampant electricity.

"Let's get to it, then." He gave me that lopsided smile that I loved, a hint of dimple flashing from his cheek, and I knew in that moment that everything had ended up exactly how it was supposed to be. Chasing the career I loved, with the man of my dreams by my side.

Twenty-Three

Epilogue

Three Months Later

I t was a Saturday afternoon, and my latest group of art students filed out of the classroom, hanging their smocks on the hooks by the door one by one as they went. They were all five- and six-year-olds, and I had been pleasantly surprised by how well they were drawing for such a young age group. I circled the room one last time making sure each piece had the student's name penciled in the bottom before I removed them from the easels, so they'd be able to continue during next week's class.

Once I had all of the projects tucked away, I turned off the classroom light and walked out to greet Finn, who was working on his laptop at the desk in the back of the store. I walked over and slid my arm around his shoulders, leaning down to where he sat, and planted a kiss on top of his head.

"How's it going out here?"

"Good, really good." He pointed to the screen, where the webstore for "The Finest Art Supplies in all of Adele" was under construction. In-person classes and sales had done much better than my initial projections, but Finn was convinced we could double our profits if we offered online options, too. So, we were. He'd proven to have a sharp mind for business, and we worked well together as a team.

He pointed out a few things he'd added to the shop as I slipped my engagement ring off the necklace where I wore it for classes, and back onto my finger where it belonged.

"You have a visitor, though." He tapped me on the arm, and pointed towards the front door, where a familiar figure lingered just inside, looking up at the student of the week's canvas hanging proudly next to the front door.

"Suze?" I called as I crossed the room, and she slowly turned to face me.

"Hey, Sienna," she murmured, looking me up and down, taking in my outfit from my paint-splattered chucks up to the t-shirt which read, "Paint no thang."

"Is everything okay?" I asked, mentally bracing myself for whatever drama she was about to drag me into. Though, she'd been shockingly quiet since the night of the storm, and this was the first time I'd seen or heard from her.

She rolled her eyes. "Yes, everything's fine. You don't have to take that tone."

"I'm not trying to have a *tone*, I'm just worried. I haven't heard from you in a while, and then you dropped by out of the blue. That's all. No tone," I insisted.

"I know, you've always been the worry wart." She half-grinned, taking the censure out of the words. "I just wanted to see your place before I left." She shrugged, and gestured to the tidy rows of art supplies, and then over to the gallery entrance. "It's gorgeous, though I'm not really surprised. You have always had the knack for this kind of thing. I'm glad—I'm glad you've taken a big step. It's a good thing." She trailed off, staring at me and biting her lip.

I was stunned into silence for a moment, unused to the kind words from my sister, and then it hit me what she'd said. "You're leaving? Where are you going?"

She looked down, and scuffed the floor with the toe of her ankle boot. "I'm going back to school," she murmured. "I've been thinking a lot lately, about what I've done so far with my life—more what I *haven't* done, really—and, I think I'm finally ready. I need to take the next step for myself. I reached out to Bosch & Harvey to find out what the qualifications were to be considered for a graphic design position. They were actually great, and laid it all out for me. Bachelor's degree, though, was a sticking point. So . . . I applied. I got into a community college up in South Carolina."

"Wow, that's wonderful, Suze. I'm impressed. And you leave soon?"

"Now, actually. The car's loaded up, and I'm supposed to check in by five."

She was cutting it close, but at least she was going. She was trying to change. "Well then, let me give you the quick version of the grand tour, and let's get you on the road." I reached out and wrapped an arm around her shoulder, and then headed for the gallery.

Once Suze was on the road, I paced back to where Finn still sat, happily coding away on my website. I stopped a moment, just to take him in. Hair mussed, glasses slipped down his nose, as he tapped away on his laptop. A Harry Potter t-shirt, declaring him a Ravenclaw. He was perfect.

I stepped behind his chair and slid my arms around him, giving him a long squeeze. "I've got a sweet tooth. What do you say we swing by the bakery, and grab a treat?"

He flipped the laptop closed and stretched back to wrap his arms around me, too. "Sounds perfect. How was class, and the visit from Suze?"

"It was great," I told him as we locked up and walked out to the car. "Nina is really getting good with pastels, and John seems to have a knack for charcoal. It's impressive for kids their age. And Suze, well . . . I think she's good. She's actually looking forward, for once. It's nice to see."

"Good for her, that's great news. And as for Nina and John, well, they've got an excellent teacher," he said as he playfully bumped my hip with his, and then held the car door open for me.

He drove us to the Sweet Nothings Bake Shop, and we chatted about small things along the way. Life had changed so much in the last few months, but it was for the better. I'd turned down the assistant art director position, to focus on the shop. To my surprise, it paid off. After only two months, I was able to quit my job and go full time at the shop, focusing on gallery sales and teaching, mixed with creating my own art during the day. Add to that all the wedding hubbub and it had truly been a crazy few months, but the ease between us hadn't changed a bit. At first I'd worried that I'd get cold feet with all of the wedding planning ahead of us, but his Aunt Dolly had it all wrapped in her iron fist and well under control. She'd occasionally call and ask my opinion on something or other, but she was making sure the details came together.

The town had accepted news of our engagement with delight, and we couldn't even buy groceries without someone coming to congratulate us. For all that our small town had its flaws, it also had its benefits. And Finn was beloved, even though he hadn't realized it before. It was heartwarming to see the town's support at every turn. Only three more months, and they would all get to see us married in the town square.

I couldn't wait.

We got a prime parking spot right in front of the bakery, and a minute later the comforting, delectable scents of hot chocolate cake and cheese danish wrapped around us as we stepped inside.

"There's our favorite lovebirds!" Bea called from behind the counter and waved us forward.

Celia sat in a corner booth with the fire chief, heads bent together over a pile of paperwork and two cups of coffee.

We placed an order for chocolate-covered strawberries—I got them every time now, because they reminded me of our first date—and two coffees. We stood off to the side sipping our coffee while we waited for Bea to get them boxed up for us.

"Harold, it's simply not acceptable, as I'm sure you agree," Celia said, voice rising uncharacteristically and drawing our attention.

"I agree, Celia, but how do we fight it? The old firehouse is a part of the town's heritage, but it's also taken serious damage from that blasted hurricane. The bricks are crumbling, and as fire chief I can't deny that it's a hazard."

"Sure, for now. But it needs to be *repaired*, not torn down and turned into a box store! We have to block this, Harold."

"I'm all ears if you've got a solution. They've offered above market value for the property and made a compelling argument to the town commerce committee on bringing new jobs into Adele. They love our town as much as the next folks, but they also see improvements where we see lost history. We'd have to make a case that the old fire station be protected as a town landmark. That's hard to do, and it's a lengthy legal process. The town's legal team can't work on it, as that's a conflict of interest. Our hands are tied." Harold shook his head sadly. "I think we're going to lose the old fire station, whether we like it or not."

"Not on my watch, Harold. I know a lawyer, and for this, I'm willing to call him." She set her chin in determination, and he raised one eyebrow skeptically.

"You don't mean Lawrence, do you?"

"I do."

"You think he'll come? He's not big on visiting Adele, all the way from Atlanta."

"He'll come for me."

"I suppose it can't hurt to ask. You two do have history together. Let me know what he says," Harold said as he gathered up the mountain of paperwork.

Bea startled us from eavesdropping when she passed us a bakery box. "Hey guys, here's your strawberries. I got you some of the freshly dipped ones from the back and added some sprinkles. You know, they'd look *really* great for your wedding. We can do them as favors, too." She wiggled her shoulders excitedly.

"Ooh, that sounds amazing. Do you think Dolly would go for it?" I asked.

"Absolutely," Finn agreed. "We can call her on the way back." We tapped the rims of our coffee cups together and walked out of the shop arm in arm.

Hey, y'all! Thanks for reading. This series has a special place in my heart, and I love this little town so much. It means a lot that you've stuck around and enjoyed it with me. I haven't decided yet if there will be more books in the series. If you'd like more books from Adele, Georgia, please let me know! In 2023, I have a new series I'm sketching out, following the Ferguson Brothers. It's all sweet, handsome cowboys, and I know you're going to love them.

Keep an eye out; they'll be on the way soon! For now, I would be so appreciative if you left a review before you move on to your next book. Reviews mean the world to us authors, and I read each and every one.

Until next time, XOXO

Kristen

TWENTY-FOUR

Playlist

I Want to Know What Love Is – Foreigner

Tennessee Whiskey – Chris Stapleton

New Year's Day – Taylor Swift

My Immortal – Evanescence

Lips of an Angel – Hinder

Ain't Always the Cowboy – Jon Pardi

Someone You Loved – Lewis Capaldi

Made for You – Jake Owen

What Ifs – Kane Brown

Slow Dance in a Parking Lot – Jordan Davis

Dancing in the Moonlight – King Harvest

Stand by You – Rachel Platten

Before You Go . . .

Thank you so much for reading The Bachelor Bargain! I truly hope you enjoyed it as I enjoyed writing it. As a new author, your review means the world to me. If you would take a moment to leave a rating or review before you go on to your next read, I would be over the moon to see it.

If you'd like to sign up for my mailing list so you never miss a new release, and get fun freebies from time to time like recipes, short stories, and the opportunity to receive free ARC copies of books, you can do so here (subscribepage.com/KristenDixon)!

I am available by email at kristendixonauthor@gmail.com as well, if you'd ever like to drop me a line directly!

I also have a fun Facebook group that I share with another author, where we trade silly memes and talk romance books. We'd love to have you join us (https://www.facebook.com/groups/rathe rbereadingromance)!

Also By Kristen Dixon

Bless Your Heart (FREE!!!!!)
Thirty and unmarried in the south, can Marlie find her forever wedding date? A romantic short story sure to make you smile.

Bea Mine (Sweet Nothings Bake Shop, Book 1)
The quirky baker. Her best friend's off-limits older brother. When sparks—and frosting—fly between them, it'll be a Valentine's Day to remember.
When two stubborn southerners don't see eye to eye, it's bound to cause sparks. But if these two can't

see heart to heart, it might just be the worst mistake the small town of Adele, Georgia has ever seen. This clean contemporary novella will have you falling in love from the first chapter.

Will Travel for Love (Sweet Nothings Bake Shop, Book 2)
A small town girl. An alluring British engineer who's just passing through. Will she follow her head, or lose her heart?
Check out book two of the Sweet Nothings Bake Shop series, and see what Celia's got up her sleeve for Daphne. Or should we say, who she's got up her sleeve?

Waiting on Forever (Sweet Nothings Bake Shop, Book 3)
She's healing from the blindside of divorce. He's a small-town hero. Can they build something together, or will it all fall apart?
With the two of them at odds, tension builds in the most unlikely of ways. Will her stubborn pride keep her lonely forever, or will Jensen be able to prove he's got enough heart to share with Maggie and her daughter?

The Bachelor Bargain (Sweet Nothings Bake Shop, Book 4)
An outspoken graphic designer. The town's most introverted bachelor. Will they open up to each other, or will the town's zany attempts at match-making push them further apart?
One sunset dinner won't change a thing . . . until it changes *everything*.

The Ferguson Brothers Series (coming 2023)

About the Author

Kristen Dixon was born and raised in Jacksonville, Florida, and is happily married with two kids. She has worked as a restaurant hostess, library book shelver, ranch hand, trail riding guide, and about twelve other unrelated fields, because variety—and sweet tea—is the spice of life. Not to mention a little thing called pursuing her passion of writing. She likes to write late in the evenings and thinks baking great cookies fuels hopes and dreams.

Her books are sweet, clean, and southern with real heart. If you like a classic southern gentleman, quirky side characters, and small towns, well, y'all came to the right place. Grab some tea, pull up a chair, and get ready to sit a spell.

If you would like to get all the latest news about her works, you can sign up for her newsletter at h ttps://www.subscribepage.com/KristenDixon and as always, don't forget to Follow wherever you read books!